Acting Edition

The Lightning Thief

The Percy Jackson Musical

Book by
Joe Tracz

Music & Lyrics by
Rob Rokicki

Adapted from the Book
The Lightning Thief by
Rick Riordan

concord
theatricals

ISBN 978-0-573-70918-0

www.concordtheatricals.com
www.concordtheatricals.co.uk

FOR PRODUCTION INQUIRIES

UNITED STATES AND CANADA
info@concordtheatricals.com
1-866-979-0447

UNITED KINGDOM AND EUROPE
licensing@concordtheatricals.co.uk
020-7054-7298

THE LIGHTNING THIEF was first produced at the Longacre Theatre in New York City on October 16, 2019. The performance was directed by Stephen Brackett, with choreography by Patrick McCollum, music supervision/direction and orchestrations by Wiley DeWeese, scenic design by Lee Savage, costume design by Sydney Maresca, lighting design by David Lander, and sound design by Ryan Rumery. The production manager was Brian Lynch. The cast was as follows:

PERCY JACKSON .... Chris McCarrell
ANNABETH ....Kristin Stokes
GROVER / MR. D.. Jorrel Javier
LUKE & OTHERS .... James Hayden Rodriguez
SALLY JACKSON & OTHERS........................... Jalynn Steele
MR. BRUNNER AKA CHIRON & OTHERS.............. Ryan Knowles
CLARISSE & OTHERS.............................Sarah Beth Pfiefer
UNDERSTUDIES / SWINGS................. Izzy Figuero, Sam Leicht,
T. Shyvonne Stewart

MUSICAL NUMBERS

ACT ONE

01: Prologue / The Day I Got Expelled
02: Strong
03: The Minotaur! / The Weirdest Dream
04: Another Terrible Day
04a: She Fought Bravely
05: Their Sign
06: Put You in Your Place
06a: Clarisse Makes a Splash
07: The Campfire Song
07a: The Trident Appears / Thunder
08: The Oracle
09: Good Kid
10: Killer Quest!

ACT TWO

11: Prologue Act Two / I Ruin a Perfectly Good Bus
12: Lost!
13: A Visit With Aunty Em
14: My Grand Plan
15: Drive
16: The Weirdest Dream (Reprise)
17: The Tree on the Hill
17a: Hellevator
18: D.O.A.
19: It's the Pits
19a: Hello Hades
19b: Sally Appears
20: Son of Poseidon
20a: Poseidon Finally Shows Up
20b: Reunited
21: The Last Day of Summer
22: Bring On the Monsters
23: Bows / Exit Music

CHARACTERS

PRINCIPAL CHARACTERS

PERCY JACKSON – Son of Poseidon, a good kid with a teenage temper

ANNABETH – Daughter of Athena, smarter than you

GROVER – A happy-go-lucky satyr, like a hippie kid with hooves

LUKE – Son of Hermes, cool camp counselor

SALLY JACKSON – Percy's hard-working mother

MR. BRUNNER aka **CHIRON** – Wise centaur, part-time Latin teacher

CLARISSE – Tough jock girl, daughter of Ares

ENSEMBLE CHARACTERS

MRS. DODDS – A Fury posing as a substitute algebra teacher

GABE UGLIANO – Percy's foul stepfather

MINOTAUR – Half-man, half-bull

POSEIDON – God of the sea, salty beach bum

MR. D – aka Dionysus, god of wine, snarky camp director

SILENA BEAUREGARD – Daughter of Aphrodite

KATIE GARDNER – Daughter of Demeter

THE ORACLE – A hippie mummy

GREYHOUND PASSENGER 1

GREYHOUND PASSENGER 2

SQUIRREL

AUNTY EM – aka Medusa, avid sculptor

TRAIN CONDUCTOR

ECHIDNA – Mother of monsters

NEWSCASTER

FARMER

ARES – God of war, rock star in leather pants

BIANCA – Mysterious girl in 1930s clothes

KRONOS – A voice in a pit

THALIA – Daughter of Zeus, brave

CHARON – Ferryperson to the Underworld

JAMES BROWN

WOLFGANG AMADEUS MOZART

KURT COBAIN

JANIS JOPLIN

DJ CERBERUS

HADES – God of the dead, moody and melodramatic

When actors aren't in the scene, they form the **CHORUS**, playing the Oracle's **ECHOES**, Medusa's **STATUES, THE DEAD** in the Underworld, etc.

AUTHORS' NOTES

Our original production featured seven actors playing an entire Greek pantheon of characters; the below doubling was based on stage time and vocal requirements. For productions where cast size isn't a concern, we encourage you to cast as many actors as you wish, and experiment with doubling based on your own needs.

We also encourage you to look beyond traditional casting "types" when it comes to the characters' race, gender, and physical ability. Above all, the characters in *The Lightning Thief* are gods and heroes – and gods and heroes can look like any of us.

Our production used imaginative, suggestive props and costuming to bring Percy's world of gods and monsters to life. Part of the joy of Rick Riordan's books is the way they mash together Greek mythology and modern sensibilities in fun and surprising ways – for example, Poseidon, the sea god, doesn't wear a toga but a Hawaiian shirt. We let that mash-up spirit guide our vision, finding creative, minimalist solutions to the challenge of staging a big, fantastical world. In your own production, we encourage you to rely on theatricality and imagination whenever possible, taking cues from the show's irreverent, rock-and-roll, DIY tone.

The below doubling was used on Broadway, with a cast of seven actors:

PERCY JACKSON

ANNABETH

GROVER / MR. D

LUKE / GABE UGLIANO / ARES / THE MINOTAUR / WOLFGANG AMADEUS MOZART / JAMES BROWN / DJ CERBERUS

SALLY JACKSON / SILENA BEAUREGARD / THE ORACLE / ECHIDNA / CHARON / GREYHOUND PASSENGER 1

MR. BRUNNER aka **CHIRON** / POSEIDON / HADES / AUNTY EM / KRONOS / KURT COBAIN / GREYHOUND PASSENGER 2 / TRAIN CONDUCTOR / FARMER

CLARISSE / MRS. DODDS / KATIE GARDNER / THALIA / BIANCA / NEWSCASTER / JANIS JOPLIN / SQUIRREL

ACT ONE

[MUSIC 01: PROLOGUE / THE DAY I GOT EXPELLED]

(The **HALF-BLOODS** *enter:* **LUKE, ANNABETH, GROVER, CLARISSE,** *and* **SILENA.***)*

LUKE.
THE GODS ARE REAL.
LIKE THE GREEK GODS.

ANNABETH.
LIKE THE ONES YOU LEARNED ABOUT
BUT WEREN'T PAYING ATTENTION TO.

LUKE & ANNABETH.
WELL, THEY DON'T PAY ATTENTION TO YOU, EITHER.

LUKE, ANNABETH & SILENA.
ESPECIALLY IF YOU'RE THEIR KID.

GROVER.
THE GODS HAVE GODLY THINGS TO DO.

GROVER & SILENA.
GODLY PLACES THEY NEED TO SEE.

CLARISSE.
GODLY PLANS THEY NEED TO MAKE.
THAT DON'T INCLUDE ME.

ALL HALF-BLOODS.
YEAH, THE GODS ARE REAL.
AND THEY HAVE KIDS.
AND THOSE KIDS HAVE ISSUES!
ISSUES!

LUKE & GROVER.

DADDY DOESN'T LOVE ME
AND MOMMY IS A GOD.

ANNABETH, SILENA & CLARISSE.

MOMMY CAN'T PROTECT ME
AND DADDY IS A GOD.

ALL HALF-BLOODS.

MOMMY IS TOO BUSY
AND DADDY IS TOO BUSY.
BUSY, BUSY, BUSY, BUSY
BEING A GOD. YEAH!
YOU NEVER LISTEN TO ME
YOU NEVER LISTEN.
YOU NEVER LISTEN TO ME!
YOU NEVER LISTEN, OH.
YOU NEVER LISTEN
BUT NOW YOU'RE GONNA LISTEN,
'CAUSE IT'S TIME YOU HEARD OUR SIDE OF THE STORY.
IT'S TIME YOU HEARD OUR STORY.

*(***PERCY JACKSON** *enters.)*

PERCY.

LOOK,
I DIDN'T WANT TO BE A HALF-BLOOD.
I DIDN'T ASK TO BE A HERO, SEEKING PRAISE.
BEING A HALF-BLOOD IS SCARY,
IT MOSTLY GETS YOU KILLED IN VERY NASTY WAYS.

I DIDN'T WANT TO CAUSE TROUBLE, TROUBLE,
I'M LESS A PLAYER AND MORE THE PLAYED.
AND HONESTLY, I'D TOTALLY BE FINE,
IF I COULD MAKE IT TO THE NEXT GRADE,
NEXT GRADE.

WASN'T THE NASTY BREATH OF MY STEPDAD,
IT WAS DANGER THAT I SMELLED,
THE DAY IT ALL WENT DOWN:
THE DAY I GOT EXPELLED!

Maybe you don't know what a half-blood is, because your life is normal and happy and not constantly in danger. But my life...?

(The **CHORUS** *creates the tableau of a class field trip at a history museum.)*

Let me set the scene:

WE WERE ON THIS FREAKY FIELD TRIP.

CHORUS.

FREAKY TRIP...

PERCY.

THAT'S WHEN THIS STORY SHOULD PROBABLY START.

CHORUS.

OOH

ALL.

WE WERE GEEKING OUT ON ANCIENT GREEK,
AT THE NEW YORK METROPOLITAN MUSEUM OF ART!

PERCY.

WE STOPPED BY ALL THE STATUES
AND LEARNED ABOUT THE GODS,
FROM MR. BRUNNER
AND MY SUBSTITUTE, MRS. DODDS,

PERCY.	**CHORUS.**
HADN'T DONE, NOTHIN' WRONG,	OOH, OOH
WASN'T RUDE, HADN'T REBELLED!	AHH!
ON THE DAY IT ALL WENT DOWN:	ON THE DAY IT ALL WENT DOWN:

PERCY.

THE DAY I GOT EXPELLED!

*(***MR. BRUNNER***, a distinguished Latin teacher in a wheelchair, lectures.* **MRS. DODDS***, the weird substitute, lurks like a vulture by his side.)*

MR. BRUNNER. The Greek Gods! Almighty titans of earth, sea, and sky! But even they were children once. And they didn't have it easy! Their father, Kronos –

MRS. DODDS. *(Suddenly ominous.)*
KRONOS!

MR. BRUNNER. – feared the day his children would inherit the earth. So what did he do? Anyone? Anyone?

MRS. DODDS. *(Gleefully.)* He ate them!

MR. BRUNNER. Ah... Thank you, Mrs. Dodds. But! One child, Zeus, escaped, and devised a plan to rescue his brothers and sisters! He tricked Kronos –

MRS. DODDS.
KRONOS!

MR. BRUNNER. – into eating a rock. And what did Kronos do? Anyone? Any *student*?

MRS. DODDS. He vomited them up!

PERCY.
WHAA?!
I DIDN'T REALLY GET THE STORY.
AT LEAST IT WASN'T BORING, AS I'D FEARED.
BUT IS IT ME, OR IS GREEK MYTHOLOGY
NOT DEEPLY WEIRD?
I DIDN'T WANT TO PAY ATTENTION,

CHORUS.
PAY ATTENTION!
PAY ATTENTION!

PERCY.
THOUGH NOW I WISH THAT I HAD TAKEN NOTES.
BUT MY FOCUS IS IN QUESTION,
AND GODS AND INDIGESTION
CAUSED A GROAN FROM ALL OUR THROATS.

(The class groans, **GROVER** *lets out a goat bleat.)*

Dude, what was that?

GROVER. Nothing.

PERCY.

MY BEST FRIEND WAS ACTING STRANGE,
AT WHICH HE SO EXCELLED.

ALL.

THE DAY IT GOT INTENSE

PERCY.

THE DAY I GOT EXPELLED!

Why do you have peanut butter in your hair?

GROVER. Ask Nancy Bobofit. She's a monster! Not literally. I don't think.

PERCY. She threw a peanut butter sandwich at you?

GROVER. She threw a peanut butter sandwich at YOU. I stopped it. With my head.

PERCY. Grover, you're a good friend.

GROVER.

DUDE. I'M YOUR ONLY FRIEND.

MRS. DODDS.

PERCY JACKSON!!!

PERCY.

I KNEW SOMETHING WAS UP
WHEN I HEARD MY NAME GET YELLED...

ALL.

THE DAY IT ALL GOT DARK

MRS. DODDS. *MR. JACKSON!* Please see me by the sphinx.

*(***GROVER** *gives* **PERCY** *a sympathetic look as* **MRS. DODDS** *leads him away.)*

PERCY. Look... If this is about Nancy Bobofit, she only hates me because I stopped her from setting fire to those first-graders –

MRS. DODDS. I have heard much about you...*Percy Jackson.*

PERCY. Really? That's very dedicated for a substitute...

MRS. DODDS. Kicked out of five schools in six years. One might question your parentage.

PERCY. Hey, don't talk about my mom –

MRS. DODDS. And your father?

(Beat. This is clearly a sore subject for **PERCY.***)*

That's right... You don't know who he is.

PERCY. How do you even know that?

*(***MRS. DODDS** *lurches toward him as a pair of bat wings emerge from her back.)*

Uh, Mrs. Dodds? You have something growing on your... AH!!!

CHORUS.

AAH!

*(***MRS. DODDS** *rises from the ground and dives at* **PERCY,** *shrieking – just as* **MR. BRUNNER** *appears and tosses* **PERCY** *a pen.)*

MR. BRUNNER. What ho, Percy!

PERCY. Mr. Brunner? What am I supposed to do with a pen –

*(***PERCY** *clicks the pen, and suddenly it expands into a sword.)*

Sword! Whoa!

(He blocks with the sword. It strikes **MRS. DODDS,** *who shrieks and dissolves.)*

...Mr. Brunner? ...Mrs. Dodds?

(But they both have vanished, and the sword in his hand is now a pen again.)

Um...

I DIDN'T KNOW WHAT JUST HAD HAPPENED.
WAS THAT ALL A CREEPY CRAZY DREAM?
MY TEACHER WAS A CREATURE,
THEN SHE VANISHED IN THE ETHER
WITH A DEMON SCREAM.
THE NEXT THING THAT I KNEW,
I WAS WHERE DETENTION WAS HELD,
THE DAY IT ALL GOT REAL.
THE DAY I GOT

*(***PERCY*** is with ***GROVER*** and ***MR. BRUNNER***.)*

EXPELLED?!?

MR. BRUNNER. I tried, Percy, but the headmaster stands firm in his decision. You were supposed to stay with the group. And this was your final warning...

PERCY. But it wasn't my fault, it was Mrs. Dodds! She lured me away, she attacked me, and... *You* saw it!

*(***MR. BRUNNER*** and ***GROVER*** exchange a look.)*

MR. BRUNNER. Did I?

PERCY. You gave me that pen! Only it wasn't a pen, it was a sword, and... What?

GROVER. Percy... We've never had a teacher named Mrs. Dodds.

MR. BRUNNER. Perhaps it's for the best. This wasn't the place for you. It was only a matter of time before –

PERCY. I got kicked out?

MR. BRUNNER. That's not what I...

PERCY. You think I'm trouble. Just like everyone else.

MR. BRUNNER. No, but... That is to say... I can only accept the best from you, Percy. Someday you'll understand why. I'm truly sorry.

*(**MR. BRUNNER** exits. **PERCY** slumps.)*

PERCY. Yeah well, I'm sorry I let you down...

GROVER. Maybe he's right. You never fit in at this school anyway. You're not exactly...

PERCY. Normal?

GROVER. Exactly! *(Off **PERCY**'s glare.)* I mean, uh... I'll see ya on the bus.

*(**GROVER** exits.)*

PERCY.

SO IF YOU THINK YOU ARE A HALF-BLOOD,
BETTER GET HEADIN' TO THE EXITS NOW.
'CAUSE FOLKS'LL THINK YOU'RE LYIN'
BETTER RUN AND DON'T START CRYIN'
'CAUSE YOU'RE MONSTER CHOW.
OR STICK AROUND
AND MAYBE YOU'LL LEARN FROM ME.
THIS AIN'T ODYSSEUS'S ODYSSEY,

PERCY.	**CHORUS.**
SO HEAR ME OUT,	OOH, OOH,
IF YOU'RE SO COMPELLED.	OOH, OOH, AHH
BUT – NOBODY LISTENS TO ME,	OOH
THEY NEVER LISTEN.	
NOBODY LISTENS TO ME!	OOH
THEY NEVER LISTEN, OH.	

CHORUS.
DUDE! YOU GOT EXPELLED!

PERCY.
I DIDN'T WANT TO BE A HALF- BLOOD

PERCY.	**CHORUS.**
I DIDN'T ASK TO BE A HALF-BLOOD	EXPELLED!
EXPELLED!	EXPELLED!

(We are now at **PERCY***'s home.* **PERCY***'s mom,* **SALLY JACKSON***, appears.)*

PERCY. Hey Mom. How was your day? Mine was okay. We went on this field trip, I got expelled, I saw some super X-rated art, museums are crazy –

SALLY. The headmaster called me.

PERCY. About the art?

SALLY. About the field trip.

PERCY. Are you mad?

SALLY. Well, I'm not happy. What happened, Percy?

PERCY. So first the math teacher turned into a demon, and then I had this sword –

SALLY. *(Quickly.)* You know what, it doesn't matter. We'll find another school. Again.

PERCY. I'm not a bad kid on purpose.

SALLY. Oh, baby, I know. *(Beat, then.)* How would you like to take a trip? Just the two of us.

PERCY. Is that okay with "Smelly Gabe"?

SALLY. I'll deal with your stepfather.

*(***PERCY***'s stepdad,* **GABE UGLIANO***, enters.)*

GABE. Sally! Where's my bean dip? Ya tryin' to starve me here?

SALLY. Gabe, there you are... *(This is hard to say.)* ...dear. How would you like a weekend without me and Percy in your way?

GABE. Who's gonna cook for me? Who's gonna clean?

PERCY. My mom's not your servant.

GABE. Naw, she likes doin' things for me.

SALLY. I'll give you a back rub. *(**GABE***'s still not sold.)* A... *(This is gonna be gross.)* foot rub?

GABE. *(Giving in.)* Both feet. And I ain't payin' any of that fancy tuition he wasted. It can come out that money you've been hiding from me. Yeah, I know about that. What're ya saving up for?

*(**SALLY** is embarrassed to admit it.)*

SALLY. Creative writing night classes.

GABE. Then I'm doin' you a favor. That's a waste a'money anyway. If he was my kid –

SALLY. He's not.

GABE. Lucky for him. *(Then, as he exits.)* Bean. Dip.

*(He's gone. **SALLY** exhales.)*

PERCY. Aw man, has that guy ever heard of showers? *(Off **SALLY**.)* Mom... You don't have to put up with him like that.

SALLY. It's complicated, Percy.

PERCY. You always say that. Why?

SALLY. Because the truth might mean saying goodbye to you. For good.

[MUSIC 02: STRONG]

SALLY. But maybe it's time.

I CAN'T TELL YOU ALL MY SECRETS...

PERCY.

MAYBE YOU SHOULD START WITH ONE:

SALLY.

YOU'RE RIGHT.
I'LL SHOW YOU WHERE I MET YOUR DAD,
HE'D BE PROUD OF HIS SON.

PERCY.

WHO CARES?
WE'RE BETTER OFF WITHOUT HIM.

SALLY.

NO!
IT'S TIME YOU FOUND OUT MORE ABOUT HIM.

(They move to the beach. Ocean sounds.)

PERCY. Look at the size of those waves!

SALLY. Fire's going. Someone needs a marshmallow. *(Playful.)* They're blue. Don't tell me you're too old for blue food.

PERCY. You met Dad on this beach?

SALLY.

I FIRST SAW HIM IN THE WATER,
COMING OUT OF THE MORNING MIST.
HE WAS HANDSOME, STRONG, AND BEFORE TOO LONG
YOU CAME TO EXIST.

PERCY.

AND HE DITCHED US.
NO COMING HOME FOR DINNER,
YEAH, HE SOUNDS LIKE A REAL WINNER...

SALLY. He didn't have a choice. He wanted to meet you. And he warned me things might be hard if you were... like him.

PERCY. Was he a screwup too? I'm sorry, Mom, if I was only normal –

SALLY. Hey!

BLUE FOOD ISN'T NORMAL,
BLUE FOOD IS STRANGE.
AND THAT'S WHY IT'S MY FAV'RITE,
I'D NEVER WANT TO CHANGE,
TO MAKE IT BORING ORANGE OR GREEN.
WHY BE BLAH, WHEN THERE'S AQUAMARINE?

*(**PERCY** tries to protest.)*

NORMAL IS A MYTH,
EV'RYONE HAS ISSUES THEY'RE DEALING WITH.

PERCY.

MOM –
IF YOU'RE WEIRD, YOU'RE WEAK.

SALLY.

THAT'S WHERE YOU'RE WRONG:
THE THINGS THAT MAKE YOU DIFF'RENT
ARE THE VERY THINGS THAT MAKE YOU
STRONG.
SO BE STRONG.

You'll see. You're destined for great things.

PERCY. The only thing I seemed destined for is detention.

I CAN'T FOCUS,
I SUCK AT SCHOOL.
MY A.D.D. GETS THE BEST OF ME.
DYSLEXIA? NOT COOL.

SALLY.

JUST HANG ON SON, ONE DAY YOU'LL FIND
YOU'LL LEAVE THAT BORING LITTLE LIFE BEHIND.

SALLY & PERCY.

NORMAL IS A MYTH,
EV'RYONE HAS ISSUES THEY'RE DEALING WITH.

SALLY.

AND THERE'S A PLACE YOU NEED TO GO
WHERE YOU'LL BELONG,
WHERE THE THINGS THAT MAKE YOU DIFF'RENT
ARE THE THINGS THAT MAKE YOU SPECIAL,
SPECIAL LIKE YOUR FATHER,
YES, PERCY, YOU ARE SPECIAL.

(Beat.)

LIKE FOOD THE COLOR BLUE,
ALL THE THINGS THAT MAKE YOU, YOU
ARE THE THINGS THAT WILL MAKE YOU
STRONG.

SALLY & PERCY.

SO BE STRONG.

PERCY. So what is this place? Are you sending me to summer school?

SALLY. More like summer camp. It's just over that hill, past that pine tree. I thought I'd be enough to protect you. But you deserve the truth.

PERCY. You're acting like I'm never going to see you again. If it's just a summer camp...

SALLY. Not any ordinary summer camp. Percy, your father is...

(The snap of a twig. **GROVER** *appears, rear first: we can't see his face.)*

GROVER. Baaaaah!

PERCY. Oh look, a goat. Hey little guy –

*(***GROVER** *stands up and turns around.)*

GROVER. Paaaa-ercy!

[MUSIC 03: THE MINOTAUR! / THE WEIRDEST DREAM]

PERCY. AAAH! Grover? What are you doing here? ...And what happened to your legs?

GROVER. I've been searching everywhere for you guys.

SALLY. What is it? What's wrong?

GROVER. *(To* **PERCY.***)* You didn't tell her about the field trip?

SALLY. *(To* **PERCY.***)* What happened on the field trip?

PERCY. *(To* **SALLY.***)* You said it didn't matter!

GROVER. *(To* **SALLY.***)* He met a Fury.

PERCY. *(To* **GROVER.***)* YOU'RE all furry! What happened to your legs?

GROVER. I'm a Satyr! I'm half-goat?

PERCY. *And you couldn't have mentioned that sooner?*

SALLY. Grover... Is a Fury after Percy right now?

GROVER. A Fury? Oh, no no no –

SALLY. Oh thank god.

GROVER. It's a Minotaur.

SALLY. Oh no.

PERCY. What's a Minotaur?

GROVER. Half-bull.

PERCY. Like you?

GROVER. *I'm half-goat!*

PERCY. *Well, I'm sorry if this is a lot to take in right now!*

SALLY. *Boys!* Grover, you need to get Percy to the border.

PERCY. What about you?

SALLY. You're the one it's after, Percy. *(She kisses him.)* I love you so much.

(Lightning flashes. Enter: The **MINOTAUR**. *Half-man, half-bull.)*

Run!

*(***SALLY** *stands, drawing the* **MINOTAUR***'s attention as* **GROVER** *tries to pull* **PERCY** *to safety.)*

GROVER. You heard your mom!

PERCY. I'm not leaving her!

*(***PERCY** *sees the* **MINOTAUR** *has trapped* **SALLY**. *He pulls out the pen he got from Mr. Brunner.)*

If Mrs. Dodds was really a monster, I hope you're really a sword...

(The pen expands into a sword.)

Awesome!

*(***PERCY** *runs to the* **MINOTAUR**, *wielding the pen. The* **MINOTAUR** *turns its attention from* **SALLY** *to* **PERCY***...)*

*(***PERCY** *swings the sword. The* **MINOTAUR** *blocks with his horns. For a tense moment, the two are locked in this position...)*

(But the **MINOTAUR** *is stronger. He pushes* **PERCY** *to the ground, injuring him. He advances...)*

SALLY. Over here.

*(**SALLY** steps in the **MINOTAUR**'s path.)*

You want my son, you have to answer to me.

PERCY. Mom, no!

*(The **MINOTAUR** lowers its head and charges **SALLY**. A frozen moment: **SALLY** meets **PERCY**'s eye.)*

Mom?

SALLY. Go.

*(The **MINOTAUR** attacks and **SALLY** falls, lifeless.)*

PERCY. *Noooo!!!!*

*(He slays the **MINOTAUR**...)*

I got him!

*(As he celebrates, the **MINOTAUR** Hulk-punches him to the ground. **PERCY** falls.)*

Whoaa...

GROVER. Percy! Don't pass out don't pass out dooon't paaaaass oouuuuutttt –

*(**PERCY** passes out. Silence. Eventually, he rises and moves as if suspended in water.)*

PERCY.	**CHORUS.**
IS THIS REAL?	OOH
AM I DEAD OR AM I DREAMING?	OOH
AM I UNDERNEATH THE OCEAN,	OOH
OR ARE MY EYES JUST STREAMING?	

PERCY.	**CHORUS.**
THIS IS WEIRD	OOH

(A guy in a Hawaiian shirt appears. It's **POSEIDON.** *But* **PERCY** *doesn't know that yet.)*

PERCY. Oh look, a strange man in a Hawaiian shirt.

*(***POSEIDON** *offers* **PERCY** *a seashell.)*

POSEIDON. "What belongs to the sea can always return to the sea." *(Beat.)* It's a seashell.

*(***POSEIDON** *disappears.)*

PERCY.
LIKE I SAID, WEIRD

*(***ANNABETH** *appears. She and* **PERCY** *lock eyes.)*

CHORUS.
OOH

PERCY.	**CHORUS.**
IS SHE REAL?	OOH
I MUST BE DREAMING	OOH
SHE'S FLOATING CLOSE TO ME	OOH
LIKE AN ANGEL, OR IT'S SEEMING.	
THIS IS WEIRD.	OOH
BUT A GOOD WEIRD.	
I'VE NEVER SEEN A FACE AS BEAUTIFUL AS –	AHH

ANNABETH. You drool when you sleep.

*(***PERCY** *snaps back to reality.)*

PERCY. Wait, what? Where am I?

ANNABETH. You had an accident. You're safe now. Your friend Grover carried you here, and I gave you ambrosia. It heals almost any injury. Unless I gave you too much and it kills you.

PERCY. Where is Grover? I had this dream, he was a goat, there was a bull, and my mom – Where's my mom?

ANNABETH. I should tell Mr. D you're awake. *(As she exits.)* Mr. D!

(She's gone. **PERCY** *takes in his surroundings. He is startled when* **MR. D** *enters.)*

[MUSIC 04: ANOTHER TERRIBLE DAY]

MR. D.

OH, YOU'RE ALIVE.
I SUPPOSE THAT'S GOOD NEWS FOR YOU,
BUT IT MEANS A LOT MORE PAPERWORK FOR ME.
SO DON'T EXPECT ME TO BE HAPPY TO SEE YOU.
OF COURSE, BEING ALIVE IS TEMPORARY.

So maybe if I go away and play pinochle for a few hours, things might improve. For me. Not for you. You'd be dead.

PERCY. Where am I?

MR. D.

GREAT. YOU HAVEN'T BEEN DEBRIEFED.
THIS IS WAY OUT OF MY PAY GRADE,
WHICH IS SAYING A LOT,
'CAUSE I DON'T GET PAID.

(Into his megaphone.)

SOMEONE FIND PROFESSOR "HAY-FOR-BREATH"
AND TELL HIM PETER JOHNSON IS AWAKE,
SO HE BETTER CLIP-CLOP OVER HERE!

PERCY. It's Percy Jackson.

MR. D. Whatever!

JUST ANOTHER TERRIBLE DAY
AT CAMP HALF-BLOOD,
WHERE EV'RYTHING'S THE WORST!
JUST ANOTHER TERRIBLE DAY.
WHEN YOU'RE IN CHARGE, IT'S LIKE YOU'RE CURSED.

Well, technically I am cursed. One romp in the woods with Zeus's favorite wood nymph and you're stuck running a summer camp for a bunch of needy half-bloods.

PERCY. Half-blood?

MR. D. Half-god, half-mortal. Does no one watch the orientation film?

PERCY. Did you say half-*god*?

MR. D. Yeah. And I half-care. *(Checks his clipboard.)* Who's next? Silena Beauregard!

*(***SILENA BEAUREGARD*** enters in tears.)*

Oh great, she's crying.

SILENA. I was walking in the strawberry fields with Charlie Beckendorf and we were holding hands and everything was totally normal and then I kissed him and all of a sudden he started growing sunflowers. *Everywhere!*

MR. D.

LOOK, KID, I HATE TO BE THE ONE TO TELL YA,
BUT I THINK THAT CHARLIE BECKENDORF WAS ALSO HOLDING HANDS
WITH A NYMPH THAT DOESN'T WANT TO WISH YOU WELL
TA TELL YA THE TRUTH, THE BEST THING IS TO BREAK UP WITH THE GUY!

Course who am I to give relationship advice? I'm literally the god of alcohol.

SILENA. But he loves me –

MR. D. He loves you not. *(Shoving her out the door.)* Next!

ANOTHER TERRIBLE DAY
AT CAMP HALF-BLOOD,
WHERE EV'RYTHING'S THE WORST!
JUST ANOTHER TERRIBLE DAY.
I'M THE GOD OF WINE AND I'M DYING OF THIRST.

PERCY. Wait, did you say you're a *god*?

MR. D. Dionysus, god of wine. Yeah, gods are real. Yippy skippy.

*(**KATIE GARDNER** enters.)*

Katie Gardner. I see you've injured your arm.

KATIE. I fell off a pegasus.

MR. D. You don't have flying lessons on Thursdays, you have archery.

KATIE. Those arrows are made of wood! Wood comes from trees! I refuse to participate in any activity that encourages the senseless slaughter of our arboreal friends –

MR. D.

OH GODS, GIVE ME ARES OR APOLLO,
ANYONE BUT THE DEMETER KIDS CABIN.
NOW THAT YOU'VE BLESSED US,
GO TALK TO HEPHAESTUS,
BEFORE I TAKE A KNIFE TO MY HEAD AND START STABBIN'!

And stay away from the pegasi! Girls and ponies...

*(**KATIE** exits, **MR. BRUNNER** enters.)*

Speaking of ponies.

MR. BRUNNER. Percy!

PERCY. *Mr. Brunner?* What are you doing here? This guy is saying all this crazy stuff about nymphs and gods and... What is going ON?!?

MR. BRUNNER. It's complicated –

MR. D.

OH KID, YOU HAVE NO IDEA
ABOUT THIS PLACE OR YOUR FORMER MENTOR.
I DON'T HAVE TIME TO FILL YOU IN ON THE DETAILS,
BUT LOOK, HE'S ALSO A CENTAUR.

*(***MR. D*** whips the blanket off* **MR. BRUNNER,** *revealing he has the lower body of a horse.)*

MR. BRUNNER. *(Sheepish.)* I did mean to tell you...

MR. D.

ANOTHER TERRIBLE DAY

MR. D.	**PERCY.**
AT CAMP HALF-BLOOD,	Mr. Brunner!!!!
WHERE EV'RYTHING'S THE WORST!	You're a horse!
JUST ANOTHER TERRIBLE DAY.	*What is happening?!*

MR. D.

YOU CAN HATE IT HERE,
BUT I HATED IT FIRST!
JUST ANOTHER TERRIBLE DAY,
STUCK WITH THESE RUNTS IN THE MUCK AND MUD.
ANOTHER TERRIBLE DAY.
OH GODS!
I need a drink.
ENJOY YOUR STAY AT CAMP HALF-BLOOD.

*(***MR. D*** exits.)*

MR. BRUNNER. You'll get used to Mr. D. He can be a bit... Well. He hates children.

PERCY. I thought you were a Latin teacher.

MR. BRUNNER / CHIRON. More like ancient Greek. My true name is Chiron. And my real job is training demi-gods. Half-bloods...like you.

PERCY. So everything that crazy guy said is true.

CHIRON. Do you think the Greek gods stopped existing just because people stopped believing in them? They're all around us. *(Meaningfully.)* And so are their children.

PERCY. But I'm not... I mean, this has to be a mistake. Let me talk to my mom, she'll clear this up. *(Off* **CHIRON***'s grave look.)* Where is my mom?

CHIRON. Grover said she fought bravely.

[MUSIC 04A: SHE FOUGHT BRAVELY]

But a mortal woman, against a minotaur...

PERCY. It wasn't a dream. She's really gone.

CHIRON. I'm so sorry, Percy.

PERCY. It's my fault. She was trying to protect me.

CHIRON. You mustn't blame yourself.

PERCY. You say the gods are real. So how could they let that happen?

CHIRON. I'm afraid there are some questions only the gods themselves can answer.

[MUSIC 05: THEIR SIGN]

LOOK FOR THEIR SIGN.
YOU HAVE TO BE PATIENT.
A SIGN THAT THE GODS HAVE A PLAN.
I KNOW THAT THE FUTURE LOOKS BLURRY,

BUT NOT TO WORRY,
JUST DO WHAT YOU CAN.
YES, THE GODS ARE VERY REAL,
THOUGH THEY OFTEN WON'T REVEAL
WHO THEY ARE, WHAT THEY WANT,
THEIR DESIGN.
HAVE FAITH, KEEP YOUR CHIN UP,
WE'LL HELP YOU ADJUST
AND TRUST YOU WILL SEE THEIR SIGN.

PERCY. If my dad's a god, I'd like to know which one. He's got a lot to answer for.

HE SHOWED NO SIGN
THAT HE EVER EXISTED.
NO SIGN HE MIGHT ACTU'LLY CARE.
MY MOM RAISED ME ALL ON HER LONESOME,
WHEN I WOULD REACH OUT, NO ONE ELSE WOULD BE THERE.
WELL, I WANT MY BIRTHDAY CARDS AND FISHING TRIPS,
CHILD SUPPORT, AND HOMEWORK TIPS!
DON'T MEAN TO WHIMPER OR WHINE,
THE GUY DIDN'T NEED TO BE "DAD OF THE YEAR",
BUT IT'S CLEAR HE COULD'VE SHOWN US A SIGN.

So who is he?

CHIRON. *(Darkly.)* It could be... That is to say... The prophecies suggest... *(A long beat as* **PERCY** *waits for an answer.) (Cheerful.)* But that's impossible! I'll see you at dinner, Percy!

*(**CHIRON** exits. **LUKE**, who has been watching from the sidelines, sees his chance and steps forward. He oozes bad-boy cool.)*

LUKE. Tough first day?

PERCY. Before this morning, I didn't believe in any of this.

LUKE. Believing doesn't make it easier. Trust me.

PERCY. All this time I thought my dad was some dead-beat. Turns out...

LUKE. ...he's a dead-beat god. I get how you feel. I was your age when I found out my dad was Hermes, the messenger god. You know, Old Wings-On-His-Shoes?

PERCY. Have you ever met him?

LUKE. Once.

PERCY. And?

LUKE. We're not playing catch anytime soon. Look, the gods are busy. They have a lot of kids, and they don't always care. If you're one of the lucky ones...

THEY'LL SEND A SIGN
IF THEY WANT TO CLAIM YOU,
A SIGN TO ADMIT YOU'RE THEIR OWN.

PERCY.

AND IF THEY DON'T?

LUKE.

THEN NO ONE CAN BLAME YOU
FOR HOLDING A GRUDGE,
SO, HEY,

(Laughs.)

YOU'RE NOT ALONE.

I'm Luke. I'm gonna be your counselor. The Hermes cabin takes anyone who hasn't been claimed. You know what that means? We're literally the reject cabin. Welcome to the dysfunctional family.

PERCY. Thanks, Luke.

LUKE. Rejects stick together. Besides, there's someone who's been waiting to see you.

*(**LUKE** leads **PERCY** to **GROVER**, pacing anxiously.)*

GROVER. I'm sorry. Satyrs are supposed to be protectors. I'm the worst satyr in the world –

PERCY. Grover. I'm glad you're here.

(The three of them share a moment.)

LUKE.

WHEN PARENTS ARE DISTANT,
OR SEEM NON-EXISTENT,
HANG ON, 'CAUSE YOU'RE GONNA BE FINE.
I KNOW IT'S A LOT TO BE THINKING ABOUT:
ALL OF THIS AWKWARD-ASS DARKNESS AND DOUBT.
IF YOU NEED A FRIEND TO HELP FIGURE IT OUT –

LUKE.	**PERCY.**
TOGETHER WE'LL SEARCH FOR YOUR SIGN!	TOGETHER WE'LL SEARCH FOR MY SIGN!

GROVER. Come on! I'll show you the amphitheater… The armory… The cafetorium…

*(**PERCY** and **GROVER** go off. **LUKE** lingers, as **ANNABETH** enters.)*

LUKE. Poor guy. He really fought a minotaur?

ANNABETH. More like barely survived a minotaur.

LUKE. You don't believe him?

ANNABETH. He shows up out of nowhere, says he doesn't know anything about us – but he's strong enough to fight a minotaur? Something doesn't add up. I just can't figure out what.

LUKE. *(Teasing.)* Well, if Annabeth Chase can't figure it out…

ANNABETH. Admit it, I'm the smartest person you know.

LUKE. Also the toughest, so I'd admit it either way.

ANNABETH. *(Flattered.)* You think I'm tough? *(Beat.)* How do you think he is at Capture the Flag?

(A whistle blows. It's now the next day. **LUKE** *and* **GROVER** *drag* **PERCY** *onto the stage.)*

CLARISSE.

CAPTURE THE FLAG!

PERCY. What's going on? And are you ever going to wear pants again?

GROVER. Nope!

LUKE. *(Hands* **PERCY** *a sword.)* You're going to need this.

PERCY. It's a sword.

LUKE. Haven't you played Capture the Flag before?

PERCY. Not with swords.

*(**PERCY** swooshes the sword* Star Wars *style.)*

ANNABETH. It's not a lightsaber.

PERCY. You're my dream girl! I mean...the girl I saw... when I was dreaming...

ANNABETH. *(To* **GROVER**.*)* Are you sure he doesn't have a concussion?

LUKE. This is Annabeth. Our cabins are on the same team. See, cabins are grouped by parent. And each cabin has certain...gifts. I figure, if we find what you're good at, maybe that'll give us a clue about your dad.

PERCY. I don't have any gifts.

ANNABETH. You have ADHD, right? Dyslexia too?

PERCY. Yeah, but –

ANNABETH. Letters float off the page when you read because your mind is hardwired for ancient Greek. And the ADHD – you're impulsive, you can't sit still in class. Those are your battlefield reflexes.

PERCY. So who's *your* dad?

ANNABETH. He's a history professor.

PERCY. He's human? But I thought...

ANNABETH. My *mom* is Athena. Goddess of wisdom. Sexist much?

PERCY. No! I mean, I love girls! I mean... I think they're really...nice!

ANNABETH. Capture the Flag isn't about being nice. It's about proving to the gods that we're tough, powerful and victorious in battle!

PERCY. She's kind of intense.

GROVER. You should see the captain of the other team.

PERCY. Who's the captain of the other team?

*(***CLARISSE** *appears.)*

CLARISSE. *I am.*

[MUSIC 06: PUT YOU IN YOUR PLACE]

PERCY. Ahh!

LUKE. Meet Clarisse, the daughter of Ares, god of war.

CLARISSE. You got a problem with that? Prepare to be pulverized – *newbie.*

(To **PERCY.***)*

YOU WANNA KNOW WHOSE HOUSE YOU'RE FIGHTING FOR:
THE GOD OF STRATEGY, THE GOD OF WAR,
THE GOD OF WATER, OR THE GOD OF DEATH
BEFORE YOU TAKE YOUR FINAL BREATH.

(To **LUKE.***)*

GOD OF MESSENGERS, GO TAKE A NOTE:

CLARISSE. *(To everyone.)*

YOU GONNA DROWN, YOU AIN'T GONNA FLOAT,
YOU GONNA LOSE, YEAH YOU MISSED THE BOAT.
IT'S GONNA BE BLOODY MURDER SHE WROTE!

I'LL PUT YOU IN,
I'LL PUT YOU IN,
I'LL PUT YOU IN YOUR PLACE.

I'LL PUT YOU IN,
I'LL PUT YOU IN,
I'LL PUT YOU IN YOUR PLACE.

PERCY. We have to beat *her*?

ANNABETH. Don't worry. Athena always has a plan.

EV'RY DEMI HAS A SPECIAL SKILL:

PERCY, GROVER & LUKE.

SPECIAL SKILL...

ANNABETH.

SPEED OR BRAINS OR THE
STRENGTH OF WILL.

PERCY, GROVER & LUKE.

STRENGTH OF WILL...

ANNABETH.

BUT SHE, SHE'S GONNA TAKE A SPECIAL SPILL –
RIGHT TO THE BOTTOM OF THE BIGGEST HILL.

CLARISSE.

DON'T MEAN TO BOAST, I DON'T MEAN TO BRAG,

CLARISSE.

BUT YOU LOSERS ARE A
TOTAL DRAG.

SILENA & CLARISSE'S TEAM.

Losers!

CLARISSE.

I FEEL YOUR SPIRITS STARTING TO SAG,
SHE COULD CAPTURE YOUR HEART,
I'M GONNA C'-C'-C'-C'-C' CAPTURE THE FLAG!

ANNABETH.
I'LL PUT YOU IN,
I'LL PUT YOU IN,

CLARISSE & ANNABETH.
I'LL PUT YOU IN YOUR PLACE!

CLARISSE.
I'LL PUT YOU IN,

ANNABETH.
I'LL PUT YOU IN,

CLARISSE.
I'LL PUT YOU IN,

ANNABETH.
I'LL PUT YOU IN,

CLARISSE & ANNABETH.
I'LL PUT YOU IN YOUR PLACE!

GROVER.
OW, OW, OW MY FACE...

ANNABETH. All right, team. Let's talk strategy. Hermes kids are fast, so Luke?

LUKE. Actually, that's a stereotype – foot brigade, got it.

ANNABETH. Grover? Satyrs are creatures of Pan – god of the wild. You know what to do?

GROVER. Yep. Hide in a tree!

PERCY. What about me? I don't know my talent yet.

ANNABETH. I have a special job for you. Go to the boys' bathroom.

PERCY. And?

ANNABETH. Stay there. It's your first day. We don't want you messing this up.

ALL.

BATTLE!!!

(Breakdown! A huge swordfight ensues. Mayhem and pandemonium, all in rhythm – à la Stomp *meets* Enter the Dragon. *In the chaos,* **PERCY** *finds his way to the bathroom.)*

PERCY. Okay. Just stay here. Just stay in the bathroom, and stay out of...

*(***CLARISSE** *appears.)*

CLARISSE.

TROUBLE?
HA! HEARD YOU WERE TOUGH,

(Snorts.)

BUT YOU DON'T LOOK IT.

(Smacks her fist.)

YOUR GOOSE IS COOKED.
I'M HERE TO COOK IT.
MAYBE THE MINOTAUR DIED FROM A CASE
OF LAUGHING TOO HARD FROM SEEING YOUR STUPID FACE!

PERCY.

LOOK, "CAPTAIN CRAZY," BUT THE FLAG AIN'T HERE!
YOU GOT SOME ISSUE WITH ME, IT'S PRETTY CLEAR.

CLARISSE.

YOU FACED A MONSTER ON YOUR VERY FIRST DAY.
YOU LUCKY PUNK, NOW NEWBIE, YOU'RE GONNA PAY!
I'LL PUT YOU IN.

CHORUS.

SHE'LL PUT YOU IN,

CLARISSE.

I'LL PUT YOU IN,

CHORUS.
SHE'LL PUT YOU IN,

CLARISSE.
I'LL PUT YOU IN YOUR
PLACE!

ALL.
SHE'LL PUT YOU IN YOUR
PLACE!

(They fight. **CLARISSE** *disarms* **PERCY,** *knocking him onto a toilet.)*

CLARISSE.
I'LL PUT YOU IN,

CHORUS.
SHE'LL PUT YOU IN,

CLARISSE.
I'LL PUT YOU IN,

CHORUS.
SHE'LL PUT YOU IN,

CLARISSE.
I'LL PUT YOU IN YOUR
PLACE!

ALL.
SHE'LL PUT YOU IN YOUR
PLACE!

[MUSIC 06A: CLARISSE MAKES A SPLASH]

(A rumble, like water moving through pipes.)

CLARISSE. What's that noise?

PERCY. It's not me. It's – *THE TOILET!!!*

ALL.
OOO-OOOAAAAAH!!

*(***PERCY** *dives off the toilet as a stream of water rises from the toilet bowl...and hits* **CLARISSE. LUKE** *and* **GROVER** *run in, followed by* **ANNABETH.***)*

CLARISSE. *(As she runs out.)* You're worm meat, Jackson! Worm meat!

GROVER. Whoa, what happened here?

PERCY. I...had...an...accident?

*(**LUKE** and **GROVER** crack up laughing. They hoist **PERCY** onto their shoulders and carry him to the campfire, where other **CAMPERS** are scooping food into bowls from a cooking pot.)*

LUKE. All hail Percy Jackson, supreme lord of the bathroom!

*(Everyone cheers. They move off, leaving **PERCY** and **ANNABETH** alone.)*

ANNABETH. Not bad for your first day.

PERCY. You set me up.

ANNABETH. I don't know what you're talking about.

PERCY. You told me to hide in the bathroom. You knew Clarisse would go after me. I was part of your plan!

ANNABETH. You mean distracting Ares' best warrior so I could capture their flag? Smart plan.

PERCY. She could've killed me!

ANNABETH. The plan would've worked either way.

PERCY. I thought Athena was all about books! And reading!

ANNABETH. She is. Also battle strategy. Look, I needed that win. I need to prove to my mom I'm a champion, so I can get a quest.

PERCY. A quest?

ANNABETH. The biggest honor a half-blood can get. But it doesn't matter. No one will be talking about my victory tonight. They'll be too busy talking about yours. How'd you drench Clarisse the Beast anyway?

PERCY. I don't know, it was like the water in the toilet just responded to me...

*(**ANNABETH** is staring at him, suddenly scared.)*

What?

ANNABETH. I *really* hope that doesn't mean what I think it means...

[MUSIC 07: THE CAMPFIRE SONG]

PERCY. What? What does what mean?

*(**LUKE** and **GROVER** interrupt.)*

LUKE. Come on, grab some dinner and let the nectar flow!

*(A **CAMPER** scrapes their food into the fire.)*

PERCY. Why did she scrape part of her plate into the fire? Is the food here that bad?

LUKE. Offering to the gods. It's not enough they're omnipotent and all-powerful. They need to feel appreciated. To the gods!

*(**LUKE** steps to the fire and scrapes off his plate.)*

CAMPERS. To the gods!

*(Perhaps **LUKE** picks up a guitar and starts to play.)*

LUKE.

OH, THINGS COULDN'T BE WORSE,
WHEN YOUR PARENTS RUN THE UNIVERSE.

CAMPERS. *(Joining in.)*

OH, THINGS COULDN'T BE WORSE
WHEN YOUR FOLKS RUN THE UNIVERSE.

LUKE.

MY DAD IS HERMES, HE MESSENGERS THINGS.
YOU'LL KNOW HIS SIGN BY HIS SHOES WITH THOSE WINGS
I'D WAIT BY THE PHONE BUT THE PHONE NEVER RINGS!
OH, NO.
WHEN YOUR DAD'S A GOD, LIFE CAN BE TOUGH.
I MET THE GUY ONCE, AND ONCE WAS ENOUGH!

Annabeth?

(Flattered to be called on by **LUKE, ANNABETH** *rises and scrapes part of her food into the fire.)*

ANNABETH.

MY MOM'S ATHENA, SHE'S SMART AND SHE'S WISE.
SHE'S SWORN OFF GLUTEN AND SHE'S SWORN OFF GUYS.
BUT IF SHE CAME TO CAMP, IT'D BE A SURPRISE.
OH NO...

LUKE.

OH NO...

ANNABETH.

AND MY STEPMOM, SHE HATES ME. AND MY DAD WORKS ALL DAY.
SO I LEFT VIRGINIA AND I RAN AWAY.

PERCY. Wait, is that true?

LUKE. Everybody!

CAMPERS.

OH, THINGS COULDN'T BE WORSE,
WHEN YOUR PARENTS RUN THE UNIVERSE.
OH, THINGS COULDN'T BE WORSE,
WHEN YOUR FOLKS RUN THE UNIVERSE.

LUKE. Who's next?

(**KATIE GARDNER**, *an earthy hippie girl, rises and scrapes some of her food into the fire.)*

KATIE.
MY MOM'S DEMETER, GODDESS OF GRAIN.
SHE GETS EXCITED WHEN IT STARTS TO RAIN.
BUT PLANTING AND PLANTING AND PLANTING'S A PAIN!
OH NO.

CAMPERS.
OH NO...

KATIE.
FOR THEIR SIXTEENTH BIRTHDAY, MY FRIENDS GOT A CAR.
I GOT A FERN IN SOME DUMB MASON JAR.

GROVER. Ooh, ooh, my turn.
I'M A CHILD OF PAN, GOD OF THE WILD.
FOR THOSE WHO LOVE NATURE, THEY'RE OFTEN BEGUILED.
HE'S NOT REALLY MY DAD, BUT I'M SORT OF HIS CHILD...
OH NO

CAMPERS.
OH NO...

GROVER.
HE WENT FOR A HIKE TO EXPLORE NEW FRONTIERS,
AND NO ONE HAS SEEN HIM FOR THOUSANDS OF YEARS.

CAMPERS.
OH, THINGS COULDN'T BE WORSE,
WHEN YOUR PARENTS RUN THE UNIVERSE.
OH THINGS COULDN'T BE WORSE,
WHEN YOUR FOLKS RUN THE UNIVERSE.

(**CHIRON** *wanders over to warm up by the fire.)*

PERCY. Chiron! Who's your dad?

CHIRON. Oh! Well...

(Not in tune at all.)

MY FATHER IS KRONOS.
REMEMBER MY LECTURE,
HE ATE HIS CHILDREN.

(Long, awkward beat.)

LUKE. Chiron wins!

*(**CAMPERS** ad-lib: "Yeah!" "Gross," etc.)*

GROVER. His dad's definitely the worst!

CHIRON. He did vomit us up!

LUKE. How about you, Silena?

*(**SILENA**, a daughter of Aphrodite, steps up to the fire.)*

SILENA.

THE GODDESS OF LOVE, MY MOM'S APHRODITE.
SHE TRIES TO BE COOL, BUT MAINLY SHE'S FLIGHTY.
I'LL BRING HOME A BOY, AND SHE'S THERE IN HER NIGHTIE!

CAMPERS. *(Reacting.)*

OH NO!!

SILENA. *(Ad-libs: "She's garbage people," etc.)*

I'VE TRIED TO SEEK HELP FROM EVEN THE FATES.
'CAUSE SHE STEALS MY MASCARA AND ALL OF MY DATES!

*(**CAMPERS** ad-lib: "Percy's turn!" "Yeah, how 'bout the newbie," etc.)*

PERCY. Oh, no. If I try to sing, it'll probably cause an avalanche.

LUKE. Hey, we're all friends here. Give it a shot.

PERCY. *(Making it up.)* Okay, um...

MY MOM WAS NAMED SALLY,
SHE LOVED SCARY MOVIES,
AND FOOD THAT WAS BLUE AND –

KATIE. He's doing it wrong.

SILENA. Yeah, who's your *godly* parent?

PERCY. Oh... I don't know.

LUKE. It's okay. A lot of half-bloods never know their godly parent. Come on, give it a try.

PERCY. *(Feeling encouraged.)*

SO MY DAD IS SOME GOD. THAT'S GREAT I GUESS.
DID HE NOT WANT ME, OR NOT WANT THE STRESS?
TOO BAD HE'S THE *WORST* AND MY LIFE IS A MESS!
OH NO *(Getting into it.)*
I HOPE HE SHOWS EVEN A TRACE.
'CAUSE I'VE GOT SOME CHOICE WORDS
TO THROW IN HIS FACE!

*(**CAMPERS** cheer for him.)*

CAMPERS.

OH, THINGS COULDN'T BE WORSE,
WHEN YOUR PARENTS RUN THE UNIVERSE.
OH THINGS COULDN'T BE WORSE,

LUKE.

BUT I DON'T CARE WHERE OUR PARENTS MAY BE,
AS LONG AS YOU ARE HERE WITH ME.

ALL.

WE DON'T CARE WHERE OUR PARENTS MAY BE,
AS LONG AS YOU ARE HERE WITH ME.
AS LONG AS YOU ARE HERE WITH ME!!

LUKE. Go on. Make your offering.

(**PERCY** *steps up to the fire.*)

PERCY. To my dad. Whoever he is!

(He scrapes the last of his food into the flames.)

[MUSIC 07A: THE TRIDENT APPEARS / THUNDER]

(Suddenly there's a rumbling. Everyone reacts.)

LUKE. Check it out! The stars!

PERCY. What's going on?

LUKE. I told you, sometimes the gods send a sign.

PERCY. Is that a...fork?

CHIRON. It's a trident. It seems your godly parent has claimed you after all. All hail Perseus Jackson, Son of the Sea God – Poseidon.

PERCY. My dad's *Poseidon*? Oh *sweet*!

(But everyone is staring at him in horror.)

...What?

(*Thunder booms. Rain pours down.* **CAMPERS** *scatter to get away.* **LUKE** *goes to* **PERCY**.)

Luke. What's going on?

LUKE. Mr. D. wants to kill you. I mean talk to you.

(**PERCY** *enters the Big House [the administrative cabin] to find* **CHIRON** *and* **MR. D** *arguing.*)

MR. D. I told you he was trouble! As soon as he showed up, *I* said, "Let's turn him into a dolphin!" But noooo. You wanted to *let him in*. To *teach him*. Like THAT'S ever worked!

CHIRON. Our purpose is to keep half-bloods safe. Turning children into dolphins is hardly an appropriate interpretation of that mission.

MR. D. I don't know, he'd be a lot safer as a dolphin. We all would! Hear that thunder? Zeus knows we've got him and he ain't happy!

PERCY. Wait, ZEUS? Like, the King of the Gods? I don't understand, why is he mad at me?

MR. D. You were born.

CHIRON. Mr. D...

MR. D. No, he needs to know. Haven't you noticed that there aren't any other little sea godlings running around? No sons of Hades or daughters of Zeus? *The Big Three gods aren't supposed to have kids!*

PERCY. The Big Three?

CHIRON. Kronos' most powerful sons. Zeus, Hades...

PERCY. ...and Poseidon.

MR. D. And you know why? *Because they're always trouble.* So where'd you stash it? Better 'fess up now, or I'll get the Hekatonkheires to pat you down. He's called the Hundred-Handed One so, y'know, THAT won't be fun.

PERCY. Stash what?

CHIRON. Look at the boy, he's clearly not a thief.

MR. D. You're right, you can't fake being that stupid, unless you're a brilliant actor and I'm also the god of drama so I can tell you: he's not. But as long as Zeus *thinks* he stole it, we're all gonna suffer. So: we're all agreed. One dolphin coming right up –

PERCY. *Braccas meas vescimini!*

*(**CHIRON** and **MR. D** turn to **PERCY** in surprise. **PERCY**'s surprised too.)*

Did I just speak Latin?

CHIRON. It's been known to happen in moments of stress.

MR. D. You told me to eat my pants. *(To* **CHIRON.***)* He's got more fire than I thought.

PERCY. Wait. What does Zeus think I stole?

(The **ADULTS** *exchange a look.)*

CHIRON. His lightning.

PERCY. His lightning. *(Beat.)* Sorry. *His lightning?*

MR. D. And not some crummy tin-foil zig-zag from a Broadway musical.* We're talking two feet of celestial bronze, capped with god-level explosives. Another god can't touch it. A mortal would be incinerated. Gee, I wonder who that leaves? A half-blood!

PERCY. I didn't take anything!

CHIRON. We know that. But Zeus is the "guilty until proven innocent" type of god, and your existence alone is suspicious.

PERCY. So what happens to me now?

CHIRON. There's only one thing we can do.

MR. D. *(Coughing.)* Dolphin.

CHIRON. One reasonable thing. But it could be dangerous.

You must go to the attic.

[MUSIC 08: THE ORACLE]

Speak to our mummy.

PERCY. When you say "mummy"... That's like Old Person for "mom," right?

---

*In the life of our original production, this line changed from "off-Broadway play" to "touring musical" to "Broadway musical" as our show moved up and on. Feel free to adapt it to refer to your own production, e.g. "high school musical" or "regional theatre musical."

CHIRON. Be brave, Percy. Because if you fail... All the gods will be at war.

(Thunder! **CHIRON** *and* **MR. D** *exit.)*

(Transition to: the attic. It's creepy.)

PERCY. Is anyone up here? Hello?

CHORUS. *(As* **ECHOES.***) Hello...hello...hello...*

PERCY. Just an echo. Guess no one's here after – AAAH!!!

(A mummified woman appears: the **ORACLE.***)*

ORACLE. *Approach, child. I am the spirit of Delphi, speaker of the prophecies of Phoebus Apollo. Approach, and face your destiny.*

PERCY. I have a destiny?

ORACLE.
YOU SHALL GO WEST AND FACE THE TREACH'ROUS LORD.

ECHOES.
WEST AND FACE THE TREACH'ROUS LORD.

ORACLE.
YOU SHALL FIND WHAT WAS STOLEN, AND SEE IT RESTORED.

ECHOES.
SAFELY RESTORED...

PERCY. Really? Okay, that's great! That's –

ORACLE.
YOU SHALL BE BETRAYED BY ONE WHO CALLS YOU FRIEND.

PERCY.
WAIT, WHAT?

ORACLE.
AND YOU SHALL FAIL

ECHOES.
FAIL!

ORACLE.
TO SAVE WHAT MATTERS MOST

ORACLE & ECHOES.
IN THE END.

(Later. **PERCY** *is in the Big House with* **CHIRON, LUKE, ANNABETH,** *and* **GROVER.***)*

CHIRON. "Go west to face the treacherous lord."

LUKE. It's got to mean Hades, right?

PERCY. Why Hades?

GROVER. The Underworld is in Los Angeles.

PERCY. Actually, I'm not surprised.

CHIRON. Hades has always been jealous of his brothers. And with every war, his own kingdom expands. If he's stolen the bolt to incite a war between Zeus and Poseidon, we have to stop him. *(To* **PERCY.***)* And I'm afraid by "we"...I mean you.

PERCY. What?

ANNABETH. A hero's quest. It's only the biggest honor a half-blood can get.

*(***ANNABETH** *storms off.)*

LUKE. Annabeth's right. Your dad needs a hero to clear his name. This quest could be the whole reason he claimed you.

PERCY. You mean because he needs me? Where was he when I got kicked out of school? Or when we couldn't pay the rent? Or when my mom... Forget it. I'm staying here.

*(***CHIRON** *and the others exchange a look.)*

CHIRON. I'm afraid that's not an option.

PERCY. What?

CHIRON. I'm sorry, Percy. Mr. D was right. As long as you're here, Zeus will punish the entire camp. Which means...

PERCY. You're going to expel me. Again.

GROVER. That's not fair.

CHIRON. I wish there was another way. Once again, Percy...I'm truly sorry.

[MUSIC 09: GOOD KID]

*(***CHIRON*** exits. After a concerned look back at* **PERCY, LUKE** *follows him out.* **GROVER** *is the last to go.)*

PERCY.

SIX SCHOOLS IN SIX YEARS.
BEEN KICKED OUT OF EV'RY PLACE
EV'RYTHING I EVER DO IS WRONG.
NEVER FIND WHERE I BELONG,
EV'RYBODY ON MY CASE.
THE SAME OLD STORY.
THE SAME OLD SONG:
DON'T ACT UP,
DON'T ACT OUT.
BE STRONG.
I KEEP MY HEAD DOWN.
I KEEP MY CHIN UP.
BUT IT ENDS UP ALL THE SAME,
WITH:

PERCY.	**CHORUS.**
"PACK YOUR BAGS, PERCY, YOU'RE ALWAYS TO BLAME!"	"PACK YOUR BAGS, PERCY, YOU'RE ALWAYS TO BLAME!"

PERCY.	CHORUS.
I NEVER TRY TO DO ANYTHING.	AH AH
I NEVER MEAN TO HURT ANYONE.	AH AH

PERCY.

I TRY, TRY TO BE A GOOD KID
A GOOD KID
A GOOD SON.

PERCY.	CHORUS.
BUT NO ONE EVER WILL TAKE MY SIDE,	AH AH.
ALL I EVER DO IS TAKE THE FALL	TAKE THE FALL.

PERCY.

I SWEAR, I SWEAR THAT I'M A GOOD KID.
GUESS I'M GOOD FOR NOTHING AT ALL.
GABE WAS A WORLD CLASS JERK.
DAD WAS NEVER THERE.
THE ONLY FAM'LY THAT REALLY MATTERED,
WELL, SHE VANISHED INTO THE AIR.
AND NOW I FIN'LLY FIND A HAVEN,
SOMEPLACE SAFE WHERE I CAN STAY,

PERCY.

'TIL IT'S,

PERCY.	CHORUS.
"PACK YOUR BAGS, PERCY,	"PACK YOUR BAGS, PERCY,
NOW GO, GO AWAY!"	NOW GO, GO AWAY!"
I NEVER TRY TO DO ANYTHING.	AH AH
I NEVER MEAN TO HURT ANYONE.	AH AH

PERCY.

I SWEAR, I SWEAR THAT I'M A GOOD KID.

PERCY.	**CHORUS.**
YEAH, PERCY, THAT'S A GOOD ONE.	OOH OOH
BUT NO ONE EVER WILL TAKE MY SIDE,	AH AH
ALL I EVER DO IS TAKE THE FALL.	TAKE THE FALL.

PERCY.

I SWEAR, I SWEAR THAT I'M A GOOD KID.
GUESS I'M GOOD FOR NOTHING AT –

ALL THE SCHOOLS IN SIX YEARS.
EV'RY BATTLE, EV'RY DAY.
NO ONE EVER TELLS ME THAT THEY'RE PROUD.
NO ONE ASKS ME, "PERCY, HOW'D
YOU LIKE TO COME AROUND AND STAY?"

ALL YOU GET ARE
BAD GRADES,
AND A BUM RAP,
AND A BAD REP,
AND A GOOD SMACK,
AND NO FRIENDS,
AND NO HOPE,
AND NO MOM...
SHE'S TAKEN AWAY.

(**PERCY** *feels truly abandoned, he sinks.*)

I SWEAR I NEVER STOLE ANYTHING.
I NEVER MEANT TO HURT ANYONE.
I SWEAR, I SWEAR THAT I'M A GOOD KID
A GOOD KID, WHO'S HAD A BAD RUN.
AND ALL I NEED IS ONE LAST CHANCE
TO PROVE I'M GOOD ENOUGH FOR SOMEONE

(He rises.)

I'M GOOD ENOUGH FOR SOMEONE

PERCY.
I'M GOOD ENOUGH FOR SOMEONE

CHORUS.
SIX SCHOOLS IN SIX YEARS.

CHORUS.
SIX SCHOOLS IN SIX YEARS.

PERCY.
I'M GOOD ENOUGH FOR SOMEONE

CHORUS.
SIX SCHOOLS IN SIX YEARS.

(The lake. **LUKE** *appears.)*

LUKE. Pro tip. When you're the son of Poseidon and you want to be alone… Don't go to the lake. First place they'll look. Don't worry. I won't tell Chiron you're here.

PERCY. Look at the waves. It's like the sea and the sky are fighting.

LUKE. They are. When the gods are mad, they want everyone else to know.

(He sits with **PERCY.***)*

I went on a quest last summer. My dad told me to steal a golden apple from some garden. It wasn't important, the world wasn't at stake. Who knows, maybe he thought it would be fun to watch. Or he had a craving for apples. Anyway, I got the apple, but there was a dragon guarding it. So I also got this scar. That's when I realized: the gods don't care about us, or if we get hurt. I get it. If it were my dad, I wouldn't go either.

PERCY. It's not just that. The Oracle said I'd be betrayed by a friend. That even if I found the bolt, I'd fail.

LUKE. That's pretty good, for the Oracle. Look, prophecies are weird, they don't always mean what you think they mean. And I'm not gonna say you owe your dad anything because you don't. But what about your mom?

PERCY. My mom's gone.

LUKE. From this world. But if she's anywhere...she'd be in...

[MUSIC 10: KILLER QUEST!]

PERCY. ...the Underworld. *(Beat.)*

YEAH, I'LL DO IT!
NOT 'CAUSE MY DAD NEEDS ME.
HE'S BEEN LESS A DAD AND MORE ABSENTEE.
BUT IF MY MOM'S ALIVE, THAT'S WHERE SHE'S BOUND TO BE.
I'M LEAVING NOW, I BETTER PACK.
HADES TOOK MY MOM, I'M TAKING HER BACK.

So what if no one's come back from the Underworld! I'll be the first.

*(**GROVER** appears.)*

GROVER. And I'll be second first!

PERCY. Aw, Grover, I can't ask you to come.

GROVER.

YOU'RE MY BEST FRIEND, DUDE. SO DON'T GET MAD,
BUT I SUSPECT YOU'LL NEED PROTECTING WHEN THINGS GET *(Goat bleat.) BAAAD!*
AND THIS KICKIN' QUEST MAY BE THE BEST CHANCE I'VE HAD
TO PUT MY PAST BEHIND ME. SO IF YOU HAVEN'T GUESSED
I'M COMING ON YOUR KILLER QUEST!

PERCY. *(With resolve.)*

SO BON VOYAGE AND FARE ME WELL,

GROVER.

WE'RE GONNA FIGHT EACH FOE, EACH CURSE AND SPELL.

PERCY.

WE'RE GONNA MARCH STRAIGHT DOWN TO THE GATES OF HELL!

LUKE. Underworld.

PERCY. Close enough.

I'M FIN'LLY GONNA PASS A TEST.

PERCY & GROVER.

WE'RE GOING ON A KILLER QUEST!

GROVER. Don't forget this: Official Camp Half-Blood questing backpack. It comes pre-packed with everything you need: gold drachmas, ambrosia squares, deodorant.

*(**ANNABETH** enters.)*

ANNABETH. You need me too, Seaweed Brain.

*(**PERCY** mouths to **GROVER**: "Seaweed brain?")*

If you're going to save the world, I'm the best person to keep you from messing up.

FIVE LONG YEARS STUCK AT CAMP,

UNDERNEATH ATHENA'S LOCKED DOWN CLAMP.

BEEN WAITIN' FOR MY CHANCE TO PROVE I'M CHAMP.

I'VE GOT MAD BATTLE STRATEGY, MY MOM'LL BE IMPRESSED.

I'M COMING ON YOUR KILLER QUEST!

PERCY & GROVER.

SO BLAST THE HORNS, GET THE FLAGS UNFURLED,

PERCY, ANNABETH & GROVER.

PAST DANGERS, SLINGS AND ARROWS HURLED!

WE'RE GONNA MARCH STRAIGHT DOWN TO THE UNDERWORLD!

PERCY. Luke! You coming too?

LUKE. I'm needed here. But how about something for the road?

*(He hands **PERCY** a shoebox.)*

PERCY. *(Unimpressed.)* Shoes. Awesome. *(He pulls them out. The shoes have wings.)* Shoes with wings! OK, that *is* awesome. So, where IS the Underworld?

LUKE. Look for DOA Records.

PERCY. It's a record company? Actually, I'm not surprised.

*(***CHIRON***,* **CLARISSE***, and the* **CAMPERS** *appear.)*

CLARISSE. Don't get eaten by monsters.

PERCY. Wait, monsters, who said anything about monsters –

CHIRON. Have a great quest!

(The camp waves them off.)

PERCY & ANNABETH.
SO WE'RE HALF-BLOODS, NOT GODS, BUT DEMI.

GROVER.
WON'T GO HALFWAY, IT'S ALL, NOT SEMI.

PERCY, ANNABETH & GROVER.
IT'S UP TO US!

PERCY.
SO LEMME
TRY MY BEST...

PERCY, ANNABETH & GROVER.
AS WE JOUNEY WEST...

ALL *(***CAMPERS***)*.
WE'RE / YOU'RE GOING ON AN AWESOME –

PERCY.
DANGEROUS AND SCARY!

ALL.
THRILLING –

ANNABETH.

MONSTEROUS!

GROVER.

AND HAIRY!

ALL

KILLER HERO'S QUEST!

(Thunder!)

ACT TWO

[MUSIC 11: PROLOGUE ACT TWO / I RUIN A PERFECTLY GOOD BUS]

(Start in darkness.)

BUS DRIVER. *(Voice-over.)* Attention, Greyhound passengers, we're now entering scenic New Jersey, and it looks like another pleasant – *Dear god, what are you doing with that sword?*

(We hear screams and the sounds of fighting. Lights up on a Greyhound bus, where **MRS. DODDS** *is attacking* **PERCY, ANNABETH,** *and* **GROVER,** *along with her sister* **FURIES.***)*

MRS. DODDS. *Perseus Jackson, I'd like you to meet my sisters!!*

PERCY. I liked you better when you were a math teacher!

GREYHOUND PASSENGER 1. Help, help!

GROVER. Everyone off the bus!

GREYHOUND PASSENGER 2. You know, this actually isn't the worst experience I've had riding a Greyhound.

MRS. DODDS. *Submit now, or suffer eternal torment!*

PERCY. I'm suffering now!

GROVER. I smell gas.

ANNABETH. Get off the bus! Now!

(They run off the bus – and boom! It explodes! We are literally starting the act with a bang!)

PERCY. Guys… We just exploded a bus.

ANNABETH. Yep.

PERCY. That was being attacked. By demon triplet math teachers.

ANNABETH. Oh yeah.

PERCY. *Is the whole trip going to be like this?*

ANNABETH. I hope so.

[MUSIC 12: LOST!]

HADES IS SENDING HIS MONSTERS AFTER US.
WE'RE DOING SOMETHING RIGHT!

GROVER.

ALL OUR FOOD WAS IN THERE.
ALL OUR CLOTHES WERE IN THERE.
ALL OUR FOOD WAS IN THERE!

PERCY.

SIT TIGHT.

ANNABETH.

LOOK, I MADE AN ITINERARY
FOR ANY ADVERSARY,
DRAWN FROM THE QUESTS OF HEROES PAST.
IT'S RIGHT HERE IN MY POCKET.

PERCY.

IT'S WHERE IN YOUR POCKET?

(She pulls out an itinerary. It's burned and still smoking.)

ANNABETH.

OOPS, IT GOT BUSTED IN THE BLAST.

PERCY.

WHAT DID IT SAY?

ANNABETH.
TAKE THAT BUS TO LOS ANGELES.

PERCY.
WE'RE NOT ON THE BUS.

ANNABETH.
I KNOW.

GROVER.
TO LOS ANGELES.

PERCY.
WE BLEW UP THE BUS.

ANNABETH.
I KNOW.

GROVER.
TO LOS ANGELES.

PERCY.
SO WHAT ARE WE SUPPOSED TO DO?!

ANNABETH.
WAIT FOR ANOTHER BUS?

PERCY.
WHAT IF WE BLOW UP THAT ONE TOO!

PERCY, ANNABETH & GROVER.
WE'RE LOST IN THE WOODS,
SOMEWHERE IN NEW JERSEY
AND WE'RE NEVER GONNA MAKE IT TO L.A.!
WE'RE LOST!

ANNABETH.
AND IT'S COLD.

GROVER.
AND IT WON'T STOP RAINING.

PERCY.
LET'S JUST GO.

GROVER.
NO! NOT THAT WAY!

ANNABETH.
NO BACKUP PLAN.

GROVER.
NO FOOD.

PERCY.
NO PHONE.

PERCY, ANNABETH & GROVER.
NO ADULT SUPERVISION.
WE'RE LOST IN THE WOODS,
AND WE'LL NEVER LEAVE NEW JERSEY
IF NONE OF US ARE MAKING A DECISION.

GROVER.
IT'S NOT SAFE TO STAY OUT HERE IN THE OPEN,
WHEN MONSTERS ARE HOPIN' TO EAT US ALIVE.

PERCY.
HOW DO THEY KNOW WHERE WE ARE,
WHEN WE DON'T EVEN KNOW?
HOW ARE WE GONNA SURVIVE?

ANNABETH.
IT'S YOUR SMELL.

PERCY.
I DON'T SMELL.

GROVER.
DUDE. LIKE, LISTEN, PLEASE.
HALF-BLOODS TO MONSTERS
SMELL LIKE MICKEY D'S.

PERCY.
WE SMELL?

GROVER.
LIKE TACOS OR TAKE-OUT VIETNAMESE.

ANNABETH.
SO HOPEFULLY THEY JUST ATE.

PERCY.
FANTASTIC, GANG.
WELL, I DON'T WANT TO DIE IN THE GARDEN STATE!

PERCY, ANNABETH & GROVER.
WE'RE LOST IN THE WOODS,
SOMEWHERE IN NEW JERSEY
AND WE'RE NEVER GONNA MAKE IT TO L.A.!
WE'RE LOST!
AND IT'S DARK.
AND I THINK THAT SOMETHING'S MOVING!!

(Hysterical.)

AND I THINK IT'S COMING THIS WAY!

(A noise.)

ANNABETH. Is it a monster?

(A **SQUIRREL** *appears.)*

GROVER. It's a squirrel.

*(**GROVER** begins talking to the squirrel.)*

SQUIRREL. SQUEEK, SQUEEK, SQUEEK, SQUEEK, SQUEEK, SQUEEK, SQUEEK, SQUEEK, SQUEEK...

(The **SQUIRREL** *squeaks continually over the following.)*

PERCY. Dude, are you talking to a squirrel?

GROVER. Satyr powers. Be nice. This squirrel knows every corner of these woods. Maybe he can help us.

PERCY. Really? Because I think that seems kinda...*nuts.*

(Music out. **GROVER** *and the squirrel glare at* **PERCY.***)*

GROVER. You hurt his feelings. Tell the squirrel you're sorry.

PERCY. I'm not saying sorry to a squirrel.

ANNABETH. He's very sorry. *(To* **PERCY.***)* Tell the squirrel you're sorry, Percy.

(The **SQUIRREL** *growls ferociously.)*

PERCY. Okay, okay, I'm sorry!

(Music back. The **SQUIRREL** *and* **GROVER** *chatter.)*

SQUIRREL. SQUEEK, SQUEEK, SQUEEK, SQUEEK, SQUEEK, SQUEEK.

PERCY. What is he saying?

GROVER. He says he knows where we are.

PERCY. Where are we?

GROVER. He says:

WE'RE LOST IN THE WOODS
SOMEWHERE IN NEW JERSEY
AND WE'RE NEVER GONNA MAKE IT TO LA

Thanks buddy.

SQUIRREL. SQUEEK, SQUEEK.

(The **SQUIRREL** *runs off.)*

(Boom! A thunderstorm starts.)

PERCY. I think the gods are trying to tell me they hate me.

ANNABETH. You *think*?!?

PERCY.

HUNGRY MONSTERS ON THE GROUND.

ANNABETH.

ANGRY GODS ARE IN THE SKY.

GROVER.

NO SAFE PLACES TO BE FOUND.

PERCY, ANNABETH & GROVER.

WANNA RUN, WANNA CRY.

PERCY.

CAN'T GO BACK TO ANY HOME.

ANNABETH.

CAMP IS WAY TOO FAR AWAY.

GROVER.

CAN'T PROTECT MY ONLY FRIENDS.

PERCY & ANNABETH.

NO PLACE TO GO, NO PLACE

(Suddenly very intense.)

GROVER.

TO STAY!

PERCY & ANNABETH.

WE'RE LOST IN THE WORLD,

PERCY, ANNABETH & GROVER.

AND THE WORLD IS FREAKING AWFUL,
AND WE'RE NEVER GONNA MAKE IT TO LA!
WE'RE LOST,
WE'RE JUST KIDS,
WE'RE ALONE,
THIS IS IMPOSSIBLE.
WHO PUT THE FATE OF THE WORLD
IN THE HANDS OF
THREE UNPREPARED
SCARED HALF-BLOODS?
IT'S CRAZY!

ANNABETH.

SO PICK A DIRECTION.

GROVER.

IT'S YOUR QUEST.

PERCY.
A DIRECTION.

ANNABETH.
WE TRUST YOU.

GROVER.
A DIRECTION.

PERCY.
A DIRECTION?!?!

ANNABETH.
A DIRECTION!
WHATEVER YOU DECIDE.

PERCY.
WHATEVER I DECIDE?!

GROVER.
WHATEVER, DUDE, DECIDE!

PERCY. Uh, there. I have a good feeling about there.

*(***AUNTY EM** *appears. She wears sunglasses and a* Grey Gardens*-style headscarf hiding her hair.)*

AUNTY EM.
CHILDREN! COME INSIDE!

(Thunder!)

PERCY. Hello, ma'am.

AUNTY EM. It's too late to be out all alone. Where are your parents?

[MUSIC 13: A VISIT WITH AUNTY EM]

GROVER. Trust me. If we told you...you wouldn't believe it.

PERCY. We're fine, ma'am, we're just... Camping.

AUNTY EM. In a storm like this? Poor dears! Aunty Em will find you a place to stay.

PERCY. She seems nice.

(They follow her in. The **CHORUS** *acts as statues.)*

Wow. Did you make all these statues yourself?

AUNTY EM. Everyone needs a hobby.

GROVER. That one looks like my Uncle Ferdinand.

ANNABETH. I have a weird feeling about this.

AUNTY EM. What did you say?

PERCY. She said, we really appreciate this.

AUNTY EM. It's no trouble at all. I've been ever so lonely. I had a boyfriend once. Sisters too. But a wicked woman ruined my life, and ever since then, no one seems to want to see me.

ANNABETH. *(Barely listening.)* Yeah, that's interesting. *(To the gang.)* We're leaving. Now.

*(***AUNTY EM** *stiffens. There's something about* **ANNABETH** *that rubs her the wrong way.)*

AUNTY EM. Wait. *(A snake-like hissing from the* **CHORUS***.)* Your eyes are quite unique, my dear.

ANNABETH. ...Really?

GROVER. *(Re: Uncle Ferdinand.)* Seriously. The detail work is amazing!

AUNTY EM. They remind me of somebody. Would you mind if I took your picture? I'd like to create a new statue.

ANNABETH. *(Flattered.)* Of me?

AUNTY EM. You deserve to be immortalized in stone forever.

PERCY. You know, maybe we *should* keep moving...

ANNABETH. It's just one picture, Percy.

(The hissing grows louder.)

GROVER. It's like you can see every individual strand of fur!

AUNTY EM. *(Re:* **PERCY.***)* Why doesn't your friend get in too?

PERCY. Yeahhh, I don't think so...

AUNTY EM. Camera shy? A handsome young man like you?

PERCY. Well... I guess one picture can't hurt. Should I smile?

GROVER. *(Re: the statue.)* Interesting choice to have him screaming.

AUNTY EM. I think a natural reaction is best.

(The hiss grows louder.)

PERCY. Does anyone else hear a hissing sound?

GROVER. Yep, she really captured Uncle Ferdinand!

AUNTY EM. Who's ready for their close-up?

GROVER. Really...captured...

ANNABETH. Don't you need a camera?

AUNTY EM. Why use a camera...

GROVER. Percy! That IS Uncle Ferdinand!

AUNTY EM. *...when you have a face like mine?*

ANNABETH. Close your eyes! Aunty M! For –

*(***ANNABETH** *and* **PERCY** *close their eyes, just as* **AUNTY EM** *throws off her headscarf and sunglasses, revealing her hair is made of writhing snakes.)*

AUNTY EM. *Medussssa! And your mother and I are old nemesissss... Nemesesssss... Nemississississs... We don't like each other.*

PERCY. Annabeth, run!

(Eyes closed, **PERCY** *swings his sword wildly. Of course, he misses.* **MEDUSA** *laughs.)*

MEDUSA. *Sssssuch a brave hero. Jussst like your father. But trussst me, your quesssst ends here –*

CHORUS.

AHHH

*(***PERCY***'s sword connects and* **MEDUSA***'s head falls off.)*

PERCY. What just happened?

*(***ANNABETH** *cautiously opens her eyes.)*

ANNABETH. You can open your eyes. But don't look directly at her. She can still turn you to stone, even *after* you've chopped off her head.

PERCY. *(As he opens his eyes in horror.)* I chopped off her *head*??

ANNABETH. I should've known who she was sooner. My mom's gonna be so disappointed.

PERCY. It's not your fault.

ANNABETH. You're right. It's yours.

PERCY. What?

ANNABETH. You led us right to her!

PERCY. You told me to be decisive! Besides, you're the one she was after! She had some grudge against your mom. What was that about?

ANNABETH. *(Reluctant.)* Medusa used to be beautiful, until Athena... *(Small.)* turned her into a monster.

PERCY. She did what?

GROVER. *(Loving this.)* She turned her into a monster. *(Off* **ANNABETH.***)* Oh look a bunch of empty boxes.

PERCY. Why would she DO that?

ANNABETH. Medusa disrespected her! She was sneaking into Athena's temple to meet up with her boyfriend... *(Pointed.)* Poseidon. Yeah, Medusa dated your dad.

PERCY. Isn't that overreacting?

ANNABETH. People always de-value wisdom, she has to be tough! It's the only way to get people to respect you! I mean her. I mean... Forget it.

PERCY. Is that why you don't like me? Because our parents don't like each other?

*(***ANNABETH***'s taken aback.)*

ANNABETH. I never said I don't like you.

PERCY. You criticize me. All the time.

ANNABETH. Look. I've studied, I've trained, I've done everything to prove to the gods that I'm the best. And you show up and – You don't even know how to hold a sword.

*(***PERCY*** grabs his sword.)*

PERCY. Yes I do. *(He hits himself with his sword.)* Ow.

ANNABETH. *(She corrects his grip.)* Hands here.

(She continues to help adjust his grip.)

PERCY. I didn't ask for any of this. Gods, monsters, quests –

*(***ANNABETH*** guides him to swing the sword.)* Oh, that *is* easier.

*(***ANNABETH*** steps back.)*

ANNABETH. Now come at me.

PERCY. With my sword?

*(**ANNABETH** pulls out a knife. They fight and talk.)*

Look, you're smart, you're brave – *(As she comes at him.)* you're scary good with that knife. How could your mom not be proud of you?

ANNABETH. That's what I want to know.

[MUSIC 14: MY GRAND PLAN]

You know the only gift my mom ever gave me? A hat that makes you invisible. You put it on and no one can see you. It seemed appropriate.

I'VE ALWAYS BEEN A SMART GIRL.
ALWAYS MADE THE GRADE,
ALWAYS GOT THE GOLD STAR.
I'VE ALWAYS BEEN A SMART GIRL.
BUT "SMART GIRL" ONLY GETS A GIRL SO FAR.

YOU WIN AT EV'RY SINGLE GAME.
YOU WANT A QUEST, THEY TELL YOU, "TOUGH."
IF YOU DON'T GO
YOU'LL NEVER KNOW
IF YOU'LL EVER BE GOOD ENOUGH!

MY GRAND PLAN
IS THAT I WILL BE REMEMBERED.
MY GRAND PLAN,
JUST YOU WAIT AND SEE!
THEY BETTER WISE UP, 'CAUSE I'LL RISE UP.
BRING ON ANY CHALLENGE,
AND SOMEDAY SOON SOMEONE
WILL NOTICE ME.

PERCY. I know what it's like to not feel good enough. You know how many times I've been kicked out of school?

ANNABETH. Yeah, but when boys screw up, they always get another chance.

I'VE ALWAYS BEEN A TOUGH GIRL.
ALWAYS BEEN THE ONE NOT TO RUN FROM A FIGHT.
ALWAYS BEEN A TOUGH GIRL,
'CAUSE MOST GIRLS NEVER WIN IF THEY'RE POLITE.

SO ME, I TEND TO STAND MY GROUND.
I'VE FOUND I NEVER CAN GIVE IN.
IT MAY NOT BE MY QUEST,
BUT MAYBE IT'S MINE TO WIN!

MY GRAND PLAN
IS THAT I WILL BE REMEMBERED.
MY GRAND PLAN,
JUST YOU WAIT AND SEE!
YOU BETTER WISE UP, 'CAUSE I'LL RISE UP.
BRING ON ANY CHALLENGE,
AND SOMEDAY SOON THE WORLD
WILL NOTICE ME.

AND YOUR STEPMOM TREATS YOU LIKE SOME FREAK.
AND YOUR DAD WON'T GIVE YOU THE TIME OF DAY.
AND YOUR MOM WON'T TRUST YOU WITH A QUEST,
SO THE BEST THING YOU CAN DO IS RUN AWAY!
RUN AWAY...

BUT I HAVE A PLAN,
AND I WILL BE REMEMBERED.
I WILL BE GREAT.
JUST WAIT AND SEE.
THEY BETTER WISE UP, 'CAUSE I'LL RISE UP.
BRING ON ANY CHALLENGE,
AND SOMEDAY SOON I SWEAR,
I DON'T KNOW HOW OR WHEN,
BUT I PROMISE YOU,
I'LL NEVER BE INVISIBLE AGAIN.
SOMEONE WILL NOTICE ME.

(**PERCY** *and* **ANNABETH** *share a moment.)*

I'VE ALWAYS BEEN A SMART GIRL.

PERCY. No more fighting?

ANNABETH. At least not with each other.

PERCY. Come on. I know how to get our parents to notice us. Help me box up this head.

(**PERCY** *takes a box and shoves Medusa's head inside.)*

ANNABETH. Whatever you're doing can't possibly be a good idea.

PERCY. *(Writes on box.)* Hermes Express Shipping. To: Mount Olympus. Care of: Perseus Jackson and Annabeth Chase.

ANNABETH. The gods will think we're impertinent.

PERCY. We *are* impertinent.

(**GROVER** *enters, beaming.)*

GROVER. Guys! I solved all our problems! While you two were here not solving all our problems, that squirrel came back and gave me these!

PERCY. Three Amtrak tickets?

GROVER. Now aren't you glad you apologized? We are totally killing this quest.

[MUSIC 15: DRIVE]

GUYS *(ALT:* Y'ALL*)*, WE GOT THIS,
YOU AIN'T SHOT THIS.
YO, I KNOW YOUR TRAIN OF THOUGHT IS
THAT THERE AIN'T NO WAY IN HADES THAT WE'LL WIN.
ALL YOUR WORRIES
COME IN FLURRIES
BUT WE BESTED FREAKING FURIES!

GROVER.

LOOK AT HOW FAR WE'VE COME,
WE CAN'T GIVE IN.
IT'S ONE FOOT FORWARD AT A TIME.
DUST OFF ALL THAT GRIT AND GRIME,
WE STILL GOT A LOT LEFT TO DO,
'CAUSE PEOPLE ARE COUNTING ON US
AND I'M COUNTING ON YOU.

TRAIN CONDUCTOR. All aboard!

GROVER.

DRIVE, JUST DRIVE!
STAY AHEAD, STAY AHEAD, AND STAY ALIVE.
WE AIN'T GOT NO TIME FOR MOPING
WHEN WE'RE WORKING AND WE'RE COPING,
SO PEDAL TO THE METAL
AND DRIVE.

TRAIN CONDUCTOR. St. Louis! Everybody off!

(They run into **ECHIDNA** *with a pet carrier. Inside, we hear adorable yips.)*

ANNABETH. Look, the Gateway Arch!

PERCY. Look, a lady with a puppy! Is that a Chihuahua?

(He reaches into the pet carrier. The yips turn to snarls as it tries to bite off his arm.)

ECHIDNA. It's a Chimera.

(She cackles as **GROVER** *and* **ANNABETH** *free* **PERCY** *and escape.)*

ANNABETH.

THAT WAS FREAKY,

PERCY.

THAT WAS SCARY.

GROVER.

YO, GUYS ARE YOU AWARE WE
KEEP SURVIVING EV'RY CREEPY CRAZY THING.

FARMER. Hop on my tractor!

PERCY, GROVER & ANNABETH.

LIKE AN ARROW FROM ORION,
KEEP ON STRAIGHT
AND KEEP ON TRYIN'
NO FATES ARE EVER GONNA CUT OUR STRING.

(A **NEWSCASTER** *reports live from a storm.)*

NEWSCASTER. As you can see, Bob, we've got thunder and flooding and hurricane-level winds. We urge all citizens to stay off the road and *DON'T* –

PERCY, ANNABETH & GROVER.

DRIVE,
JUST DRIVE!
STAY AHEAD, STAY AHEAD, AND STAY ALIVE.
THE WEATHER MAY BE STORMY
BUT THE ROAD IS STILL BEFORE ME,
SO PEDAL TO THE METAL
AND DRIVE.

FARMER. Bye kids!

*(***PERCY, ANNABETH,** *and* **GROVER** *study a map in a diner booth.)*

ANNABETH. Here's the problem. Public transportation is suspended due to the storm, and if we get on a plane, Zeus will strike us right out of the sky.

PERCY. Do we have enough drachmas for an Uber?

GROVER. We don't even have enough drachmas for a veggie burger.

PERCY. If you hadn't bought all those dam snacks –

GROVER. It was the Hoover Dam! And I was hungry!

(They all lapse into ad-lib fighting: "If you hadn't..." "That is so Poseidon!" "What does that even mean?")

PERCY. Wait. Why are we fighting?

*(**ARES** appears, a war god in biker gear.)*

ARES. I have that effect. Ares, god of war. Maybe you've met my daughter – Clarisse?

(They all draw their weapons.)

Relax, I come in peace. I hear you runts are headed to Hades. But you'll never make it on public transportation. I can take you as far as Vegas. Y'all cool with motorcycles, right?

*(**PERCY, ANNABETH,** and **GROVER** convene.)*

PERCY. What do you think? Can we trust this guy?

GROVER.
IT'S ONE FOOT FORWARD AT A TIME.

PERCY.
DUST OFF ALL THAT GRIT AND GRIME?

ANNABETH.
WE STILL –

PERCY, ANNABETH & GROVER.
GOT A LOT LEFT TO DO,
'CAUSE PEOPLE ARE COUNTING ON US
AND I'M COUNTING ON YOU.

(A motorcycle revs up. They ride it.)

PERCY, ANNABETH, GROVER & ARES.
DRIVE,

ARES.
DRIVE,

PERCY, ANNABETH, GROVER & ARES.
JUST DRIVE!
STAY AHEAD, STAY AHEAD, AND STAY ALIVE.

ARES.
THE ROAD, IT OFFERS FREEDOM,
AS FOR RULES, HELL, WE DON'T NEED 'EM

PERCY, ANNABETH, GROVER & ARES.
SO PEDAL TO THE METAL
AND DRIVE.

PERCY.	**CHORUS.**
I NEVER DREAMED THAT I COULD DO THIS.	AHH AHH
NEVER FELT LIKE I WAS WORTH A DAMN.	AHH AHH
BUT I, I'M SORTA GETTING THROUGH THIS.	AHH AHH
I MEAN, WHA? I MEAN, LOOK AT WHERE I AM!	AHH

(He swallows a bug and chokes.) Bug! Bug! I swallowed a bug!

ARES. Vegas, baby!

GROVER. Thanks for the ride.

(They climb off.)

ARES. Forgetting something? *(Ares tosses* **PERCY** *his backpack.)* This is where I get off.

(He screeches away.)

GROVER. That guy is so cool.

ANNABETH. Okay gang, we'll be in L.A. tomorrow. But tonight we need a place to sleep.

PERCY. How about here? The Lotus Hotel.

ANNABETH. You're joking, right? In *The Odyssey*, if you went to sleep in a lotus bed, one night could last one hundred years!

PERCY. I'm sure that's irrelevant.

(He stops **BIANCA**, *dressed in 1930s fashion.)*

Excuse me, miss, how long have you been at this hotel?

BIANCA. Why, my brother and I arrived just yesterday: May First... *(***PERCY** *looks at* **ANNABETH**: *See?)* 1939.

(They can't get away fast enough.)

PERCY. We can sleep on the road.

PERCY, ANNABETH & GROVER.

DRIVE, JUST DRIVE!
STAY AHEAD, DON'T GET DEAD, AND STAY ALIVE

GROVER.

WITH THE WIND UPON OUR FACES,
WE'RE GETTING ALL THE PLACES!

ANNABETH.

NO MAJOR FENDER BENDERS,
NOW WE'RE LOOKING LIKE CONTENDERS!

PERCY.

THE ORACLE CAN CAN IT,
I'LL SAVE MY MOM THEN SAVE THE PLANET!

PERCY, ANNABETH & GROVER.

SO PEDAL TO THE METAL AND –

PERCY. Look, a bus to Los Angeles!

ANNABETH. Are you sure that's a good idea?

PERCY. This one we just won't blow up.

PERCY, ANNABETH & GROVER.
DRIVE!

(They collapse on the bus, exhausted.)

ANNABETH. It's crazy to think this time tomorrow, we'll be at the Underworld.

GROVER. Yeah, then all we have to do is find Hades, get the bolt back, and stop a bunch of gods from starting a war. We have a plan for that, right?

PERCY. We'll figure it out in the morning. I'm about ready to pass out –

[MUSIC 16: THE WEIRDEST DREAM (REPRISE)]

paaassss ouutttt paaaaaaaassssss ouuuuuuuttttt...

(Creepy music. **PERCY** *wakes up in the Underworld.)*

THIS IS STRANGE.
I THINK I MUST BE DREAMING?
I'M IN SOME KIND OF CAVERN,
AT LEAST THAT'S HOW IT'S SEEMING.
THIS IS...

Scary.

(A large pit appears. There's something down there, speaking in a deep, rumbling voice.)

VOICE OF KRONOS. *WHERE IS THE BOLT?*

(A shadowy figure appears. It's **LUKE**, *but his identity shouldn't be obvious.)*

LUKE. The bolt is on its way, my lord. Everything is unfolding as I – as *we* planned.

VOICE OF KRONOS. *YOU FALTER.*

LUKE. It's nothing. *(Beat.)* The delivery requires certain... sacrifices.

VOICE OF KRONOS. *SACRIFICE IS NECESSARY TO REMAKE THE WORLD. REMEMBER WHAT THESE GODS HAVE DONE. REMEMBER THALIA. AND WHEN I AM FREE – WAIT. SOMEONE IS HERE, LISTENING EVEN AS HE DREAMS. HELLO, PERSEUS JACKSON.*

(It laughs, horribly, as we hear the sound of something rising from the pit.)

PERCY. AAH!!

*(**PERCY** bolts awake, still on the bus next to **GROVER**.)*

GROVER. You really do drool in your sleep.

PERCY. Wha? What happened?

GROVER. You were screaming. It was waking up the other passengers. Well, not Annabeth.

ANNABETH. *(Talking in her sleep.)* Mom? You remembered my birthday...

PERCY. I had this dream. I was at the edge of a pit, and the thief was there. He was talking about the bolt.

GROVER. That must've been Hades.

PERCY. He wasn't alone. There was some *thing* in the pit. It told him to remember...Thalia?

*(Off **GROVER**.)* What?

GROVER. I haven't heard that name in a long time.

PERCY. You know who she is?

GROVER. She was my friend.

[MUSIC 17: THE TREE ON THE HILL]

(He hesitates.) I should've told you. I thought, if I did, you'd never want me on this quest. If you knew what a failure I really am. Ask Annabeth. She knows.

THERE'S A TREE ON A HILL, UP ON HALF-BLOOD HILL,
THAT WATCHES OVER US, SILENT AND STILL.
AND NO ONE AT CAMP IS SAFE UNTIL
WE CAN SEE THE TREE ON THE HILL.

This was way before I met you. Chiron sent me to escort three half-bloods to camp. Two were runaways. One was Annabeth. The other was Luke.

*(**ANNABETH** and **LUKE** appear, as kids.)*

The third was Thalia.

*(They're joined by **THALIA**, a young daughter of Zeus.)*

GROVER.	**THALIA, LUKE & ANNABETH.**
Tough girl.	OOH –

GROVER. Like her dad...

Zeus.

PERCY. I thought I was the only kid of the Big Three Gods.

GROVER. You are now. We'd almost made it to camp, but I got nervous. And we got lost. By the time we found the hill...

(A shadow of a huge Cyclops appears.)

Something found us.

GROVER.	**CHORUS.**
AND THERE ON THE HILL, UP ON HALF-BLOOD HILL	AH

GROVER.	**CHORUS.**
A COLD WIND BLEW, DARK AND CHILL;	AH
	AH
FOR NOTHING WOULD SLAKE ITS WRATHFUL WILL.	AH

GROVER.

WE HAD TO MAKE A STAND –

(Reluctantly, **GROVER** *leads* **LUKE** *and* **ANNABETH** *to safety as* **THALIA** *fights the Cyclops.)*

AND MAYBE IF I'D BEEN A LITTLE BIT BRAVER.
MAYBE IF I'D STAYED BEHIND TO FIGHT.
BUT "MAYBE" DOESN'T LET ME GO BACK AND SAVE HER.
"MAYBE" DOESN'T MAKE IT ALRIGHT.

Thalia saved us. We only survived because she stayed to hold off the monsters. She paid for her sacrifice with her life. That's when Zeus showed up.

PERCY. And saved her... Right?

GROVER. It was too late for that.

GROVER.	**THALIA.**
As she died, he turned her	OOH –
into a tree,	AHH –

GROVER. So she could stand protecting us, forever.

The way I couldn't do for her.

(We see **LUKE** *and* **ANNABETH** *react in flashback as* **THALIA** *becomes a tree.)*

THERE'S A TREE ON A HILL, UP ON HALF-BLOOD HILL,
THAT PROTECTS US ALL, AND ALWAYS WILL.
AND IT'S THERE REMINDING ME
OF ALL I FAILED TO BE
THE TREE ON THE HILL.

I don't know why you heard her name in your dream. But I know what it means. If we fail this quest, it's gonna be my fault.

(We see **ANNABETH** *has been awake and watching.)*

ANNABETH. That's not true, Grover. I wouldn't be alive if it wasn't for you. Neither would Luke.

PERCY. You're awake.

ANNABETH. We're almost at the Underworld. Kind of hard to sleep.

PERCY. What if this is a mistake? We've been so sure Hades is the thief. But what if we're wrong? The Oracle told me I'd fail –

(The bus comes to a halt.)

ANNABETH. We're here.

GROVER. Are we sure we're ready to do this?

PERCY. Not at all. Let's go.

[MUSIC 17A: HELLEVATOR]

(They get off the bus and arrive at DOA Records.)

This must be it. DOA Records.

GROVER. Kinda figured there'd be monsters.

PERCY. Yeah, who knew the lobby of the Underworld would be so...

(Ding! An elevator opens to reveal **CHARON.***)*

CHARON. Dead? *(She smiles.)* Going down?

ANNABETH. *(To* **PERCY** *and* **GROVER.***)* That's Charon, the ferryman to the Underworld. *(To* **CHARON.***)* We need to get to Hades.

CHARON. You don't look dead. Read the sign. No soliciting, no loitering, no living.

PERCY. We're totally dead.

GROVER. Yeah, we, um, drowned. In the bathtub.

ANNABETH. All three of us.

(**CHARON** *raises an eyebrow.)*

CHARON. Big bathtub. Passage across the River Styx isn't free. With adults, I usually charge their credit card or add the ferry price to their last cable bill. But children… *(A grim smile.)* They never die prepared.

(**ANNABETH** *hands over drachmas.)*

Gold drachmas. *(She's shocked to realize:)* Y'all are half-bloods.

ANNABETH. Is that a problem?

CHARON. Not at all.

(They climb in the elevator.)

You know, the ferryman thing is just a day job. My real passion is music. Do you wanna hear my demo?

[MUSIC 18: D.O.A.]

PERCY, ANNABETH & GROVER. Um – *(They all ad-lib, hastily declining.)*

CHARON. I'm sorry, I couldn't hear you over this sweet-ass riff.

SEEN PLENTY PEOPLE ALL OVER THE YEARS,
FROM HEROES TO HALF-BLOODS WITH THEIR PITIFUL TEARS.
THINKING THAT THEY'LL SAVE A LOVED ONE FROM BELOW.

CHARON & THE DEAD.

OH, NO! OH, NO! OH, NO!

CHARON.
THEY THINK THEY'LL POP DOWN FOR A QUICK TRIP.

*(**JAMES BROWN** appears.)*

JAMES BROWN.
BUT IT DON'T WORK LIKE THAT!

CHARON.
SO KIDS, HERE'S A TIP:
YOU AIN'T GETTIN' OUT .
WE GOTCHA AND WE AIN'T LETTING GO.

CHARON & THE DEAD.
OH, NO! OH, NO!

CHARON.
DOWN HERE YOU'RE D.O.A.
AND YOU'RE HERE TO STAY.
YEAH, YOU'RE STUCK FOREVER,
NEVER GET AWAY.
NO HOPE FOR SURVIVAL.
YOU'RE DEAD ON ARRIVAL!

What do you think of my song?

PERCY, ANNABETH & GROVER. *(Terrified.)* It's great! / Keep at it! / Was that James Brown?

CHARON. I tried playing it for some producers but they told me the music industry is dead. I told them, "So are you." Then I dropped them in the Fields of Punishment. It's right over there.

(They hear screaming. **CHARON** *smiles.)*

Maybe death metal isn't your genre? We have all the greats down here. Mozart, Janis Joplin, Kurt Cobain. Who do you feel like listening to?

(The aforementioned **DEAD MUSICIANS** *appear.)*

GROVER. Do you have any Josh Groban?

CHARON. We will. Eventually.

I FERRY THE SOULS OF THE NEWLY DECEASED.
I GOT A SWEET RIDE, IT WAS NEWLY LEASED.
AND IF THE DEAD COMPLAIN,
I JUST TURN UP THE STEREO!

JANIS JOPLIN.

WE GET OUR KICKS ACROSS THE RIVER STYX.

KURT COBAIN.

IT'S A PERMANENT TRIP, SO DON'T TRY NO TRICKS.

WOLFGANG AMADEUS MOZART.

GENTLEMEN UND LADIES, IT'S HADES WHO RUNS THE SHOW.

CHARON. Oh look, the Vienna Boys' Choir. They crashed their bus on their way to sing for the Vatican.

PERCY. They're kids.

CHARON. They're lucky. Their voices will never change now.

VIENNA BOYS' CHOIR. Eins, zwei, drei!

DOWN HERE YOU'RE D.O.A.
AND YOU'RE HERE TO STAY.
YEAH, YOU'RE STUCK FOREVER,
NEVER GET AWAY.
NO HOPE FOR SURVIVAL.

CHARON.

YOU'RE DEAD!

(A **DJ** *with three dog heads all with floppy dog ears bobs along. Could be a dog helmet like Daft Punk. He howls and mixes a turntable with noises such as screams of pain and sobs.)*

CHARON. Who's got two turn-tables and three sick heads? Make some noise for DJ Cerberus!

CHARON & THE DEAD.

D. O. A.

THE DEAD, PERCY, ANNABETH & GROVER.

D. O. A.!
AH!

CHARON.	**THE DEAD.**
DOWN HERE YOU'RE D.O.A.	OOH
YOU'RE HERE TO STAY.	OOH
AND YEAH, YOU'RE STUCK FOREVER,	OOH
NEVER GET AWAY	OOH
NO HOPE FOR SURVIVAL.	WAH
YOU'RE DEAD ON ARRIVAL!	YOU'RE DEAD ON ARRIVAL!
DEAD ON ARRIVAL.	OOH OH!

THE DEAD.

CAN'T GET
CAN'T GET AWAY.
CAN'T GET AWAY
'CAUSE YOU'RE D.O.A., NOW!
CAN'T GET
CAN'T GET AWAY.
CAN'T GET AWAY
'CAUSE YOU'RE D.O.A.!

PERCY, GROVER & ANNABETH.	**CHARON.** *(To* **PERCY.***)*
CAN'T GET	YOU AIN'T EVER GONNA
CAN'T GET AWAY.	SAVE WHAT MATTERS.

PERCY, GROVER & ANNABETH.

CAN'T GET AWAY
'CAUSE YOU'RE/WE'RE D.O.A., NOW!

PERCY, GROVER & ANNABETH.	**CHARON.** *(To* **GROVER.***)*
CAN'T GET	YOU AIN'T GONNA PROTECT
CAN'T GET AWAY.	YOUR FRIENDS.

PERCY, GROVER & ANNABETH.

CAN'T GET AWAY
'CAUSE YOU'RE/WE'RE D.O.A.!

PERCY, GROVER & ANNABETH.	**CHARON.** *(To* **ANNABETH.***)*
CAN'T GET	YOU AIN'T EVER GONNA
CAN'T GET AWAY	BE REMEMBERED.

PERCY, GROVER & ANNABETH.

CAN'T GET AWAY
'CAUSE YOU'RE/WE'RE D.O.A., NOW !

PERCY, GROVER & ANNABETH.	**CHARON.** *(To* **ALL THREE.***)*
CAN'T GET	THIS IS WHERE YOUR STORY ENDS,

PERCY, GROVER & ANNABETH.

CAN'T GET AWAY
CAN'T GET AWAY

PERCY, GROVER & ANNABETH.	**CHARON.** *(To* **ALL THREE.***)*
'CAUSE YOU'RE/WE'RE D.O.A.	TODAY!

ALL.

D.O.A.!

CHARON. Enjoy eternity.

[MUSIC 19: IT'S THE PITS]

*(***CHARON** *and* **THE DEAD** *vanish.* **PERCY, ANNABETH,** *and* **GROVER** *look around in the dark, nervously.)*

PERCY. Did she mean eternity like...eternity?

(The **CHORUS** *as* **GHOULS** *ad-lib ghoulish whispers.)*

ANNABETH. C'mon, we have to find Hades. Stay close. *(Suddenly,* **PERCY** *jerks away from her.)* What did I just say?

PERCY. Sorry, I don't know what came over me.

ANNABETH. We have to be careful. If we get separated, we may never find each other again, so – *(***PERCY** *jerks away again.)* Seriously?!?

PERCY. I can't help it! It's like my feet won't listen to my brain!

ANNABETH. Well, tell your brain to do something!

PERCY. I swear, it's not me! It's – my – shoes! They're trying to pull me into that piiiiiit!

(Sure enough, **PERCY***'s winged shoes have taken on a life of their own. They carry him to the edge of a pit.)*

GROVER. Percy!

*(***GROVER** *and* **ANNABETH** *try to grab* **PERCY***.)*

ANNABETH. Whoa! Gotcha! *(But now all three are pulled towards the pit.)* Take off your shoes!

PERCY. I'm a little – AH! – preoccupied!

GROVER. I'm on it.

*(***GROVER** *busies himself at* **PERCY***'s feet. Finally, he rises proudly, holding the shoes.)*

Chewed 'em off. *(They squirm in his hands.)* Whoa! In you go...

(He tosses the shoes into the pit. They echo as they flutter down. Silence.)

(Then: a horrible roar. The sound of something big and angry. It sounds almost like it's saying...)

VOICE OF KRONOS. *PEEEERRRRCCCCYYYY.*

(But then it's gone.)

PERCY. What *was* that?

ANNABETH. Guys... I think this pit is Tartarus.

PERCY. Like...the fish sauce?

ANNABETH. Tatar*us*. It's like the maximum-security wing of the Underworld.

PERCY. What's so bad the regular-security wing isn't enough?

ANNABETH. Chiron told you our parents went to war against their father? First they overthrew him. Then they threw him – into a pit.

PERCY. You mean that thing down there is... Kronos? But it doesn't make sense! What would Kronos want with my shoes?

GROVER. They were really cool shoes.

ANNABETH. Unless it wasn't the shoes he was after...

*(**ANNABETH** pulls off **PERCY**'s backpack.)*

PERCY. You think he wanted...my deodorant?!

*(**ANNABETH** opens the backpack to reveal a glowing lightning bolt. **GROVER** gasps.)*

GROVER. That's Zeus's bolt...

PERCY. But why would it be in my... No. You can't think – I didn't steal it, I swear!

ANNABETH. Then how did it get there?

PERCY. I don't know! How did *you* know where to find it?

ANNABETH. I didn't! It was a hypothesis! A guess! Stop looking at me like that!

PERCY. "Betrayed by a friend," how bad did you need a quest anyway?

ANNABETH. Not that bad! Look, there's something weird going on.

PERCY. Yeah. Someone's trying to pit the Big Three against each other. But it's not Hades. We need to get out of here before he finds us.

*(***HADES** *enters, with flair.)*

HADES. It's too late for that.

[MUSIC 19A: HELLO HADES]

You're as rash as your father, Son of Poseidon. And from the looks of it, as stupid.

PERCY. You know who we are?

HADES. And I know why you're here. You thought I was the bad guy. Everyone always thinks Hades is the bad guy! Maybe it's the décor.

PERCY. Look, you were framed. So was I. If you just let us go –

HADES. And why would I want to do that?

GROVER. Because...you're super chill that way?

HADES. One does not simply walk out of the Underworld! That's the whole point of the Underworld! *(Beat.)* Unless...

PERCY. Unless what?

HADES. You give me that bolt.

(He lets this land.)

HADES. I may not have stolen it. But since it's here... What do the Trojans say? "Don't look a gift god-level-explosive in the mouth."

PERCY. Why would you want to start a war?

HADES. When the gods go to war, it's the mortals who suffer...and end up here. And I do get lonely.

ANNABETH. No chance. We came here to stop a war, not start one.

PERCY. Yeah, there's no way in hell – sorry – that we're handing this over.

HADES. Not even in exchange for her?

[MUSIC 19B: SALLY APPEARS]

(He waves a hand and **SALLY** *appears.)*

SALLY. Percy?

PERCY. Mom? Mom!

(But she vanishes.)

HADES. She is merely a shade, but I could restore her. What has your father ever done for you? He doesn't care about his family, or his brother, who he never visits. He's too busy playing with mermaids, and dolphins, and thinking he's so cool in his Hawaiian shirt.

PERCY. Did you say Hawaiian shirt?

HADES. I can give you your freedom, your friends, and your mother. All it will cost is a little war. The choice is yours, Son of Poseidon. I'll give you a moment to consider.

[MUSIC 20: SON OF POSEIDON]

PERCY.

SEEMS MY GOOD INTENTIONS ALWAYS CRASH AND BURN.
EV'RYTHING I TRY TO DO WILL FAIL.

NEVER ONCE WILL I PREVAIL,
GOING WRONG AT EV'RY TURN.

*(**SALLY** appears.)*

SALLY.
WHAT BELONGS TO THE SEA CAN ALWAYS RETURN.

PERCY & SALLY.
WHAT BELONGS TO THE SEA CAN ALWAYS RETURN.

PERCY. *(Remembering.)* It's a seashell. No... It's a gift from a god.
MAYBE MY DAD WAS A SCREWUP TOO,
HIS BEST LAID PLANS ALWAYS FALLING THROUGH.
MAYBE HE DID THE BEST THAT HE COULD DO.
MAYBE MY DAD WASN'T ALWAYS THERE.
MAYBE HE NEVER KNEW HOW TO CARE.
BUT HEY, THAT'S LIFE,
AND LIFE AIN'T FAIR.
AND I KNOW RIGHT NOW THINGS ARE LESS THAN FINE.
BUT I THINK MY DAD MAY HAVE THROWN ME A LINE.
AND BETTER LATE THEN NEVER
TO FINALLY GET A SIGN!

(He pulls out the seashell.)

I'M THE SON OF POSEIDON,
AND I AM GONNA WIN!
THE SON OF POSEIDON
AND I'M DONE RUNNIN'.

Guys, I know how to get us out of here! I'll come back for you, Mom. I promise.

*(**PERCY** blows the seashell and a portal appears.)*

It's a portal!

HADES. Oh, come on!

(They go through the portal and end up on a beach.)

PERCY. We were set up. And I think I know who did the setting.

ANNABETH. But if it's not Hades...?

PERCY. Who wins if the gods go to war? Ares, the god of war. He must have planted the bolt in my backpack. I bet he's watching us right now. *(Calling out to the sky.) Show yourself.*

ANNABETH.

WELL, HE'LL HAVE TO GET THROUGH ME.
WE'LL TAKE HIM DOWN, WE WORK WELL IN THREE.

GROVER.

PLUS A HALF-GOAT WITH A GREAT GOATEE.
LET'S DO THIS!

PERCY.

SO THIS COULD BE THE END BUT I AIN'T SAD.
'CAUSE YOU'RE THE TWO BEST FRIENDS
THIS SCREWUP EVER HAD.
AND NOW I'LL MAKE THIS RIGHT FOR ME AND FOR MY DAD!
I'M THE SON OF POSEIDON,
AND WE KNOW YOU'RE TO BLAME.

PERCY, ANNABETH & GROVER.

THE SON OF POSEIDON.

PERCY.

YOU MAY BE A GOD BUT YOU'RE GOING DOWN ALL THE SAME!

*(**ARES** suddenly appears with a baseball bat.)*

ARES.

HA!
YOUR MOUTH'S TALKING TRASH,

YOU BETTER RINSE IT.
YOUR MEAT IS MINCED
I'M HERE TO MINCE IT.
I'M GONNA HAVE MY WAR, NOW GIMME SOME SPACE.
I'M GONNA WIPE THAT STUPID HEAD OFF OF YOUR STUPID FACE!

PERCY.	**ARES.**	**GROVER & ANNABETH.**
I'M THE SON OF	I'LL PUT YOU IN.	WE'LL PUT YOU IN.
POSEIDON.	I'LL PUT YOU IN.	WE'LL PUT YOU IN.
AND I AM GONNA WIN!	I'LL PUT YOU IN YOUR PLACE!	WE'LL PUT YOU IN YOUR PLACE!
THE SON OF	I'LL PUT YOU IN.	WE'LL PUT YOU IN.
POSEIDON	I'LL PUT YOU IN	WE'LL PUT YOU IN
AND I'M DONE RUNNIN'	I'LL PUT YOU IN YOUR PLACE!	WE'LL PUT YOU IN YOUR PLACE!

PERCY. There's something I can't figure out. You needed a half-blood to steal the bolt. Tell us who's helping you!

ARES. Make me. Let the slugfest begin!

(An epic battle ensues.)

ANNABETH. Percy, get to the ocean!

ARES. You think the god of war is afraid of a little water?

PERCY. How do you feel about a lot of it?

PERCY.	**CHORUS.**
I'M THE	AH
SON OF POSEIDON,	
I NEVER ASKED TO BE	
BUT I'M THE	
SON OF POSEIDON.	SON OF POSEIDON.
NOW FACE THE TIDE	
INSIDE ME!	AH! AH!

(A giant tidal wave washes **ARES** *away.)*

ARES.
NOOOOO!!!

(**GROVER** *and* **ANNABETH** *run to* **PERCY**.)

ANNABETH. That was amazing!

GROVER. That was awesome!

ANNABETH. How did you do that?

[MUSIC 20A: POSEIDON FINALLY SHOWS UP]

(**POSEIDON** *enters.*)

POSEIDON. He's a true son of the sea. And the sea does not like to be restrained.

PERCY. Dad. I mean, Lord Poseidon.

POSEIDON. You can call me Dad, Perseus.

PERCY. You can call me Percy. *(Beat.)* I got your gift.

POSEIDON. I got yours. *(He holds up a box.)* Medusa's head? Really?

PERCY. Yeahh, about that...

POSEIDON. You have a talent for getting in trouble. Like your old man. But you have your mother's strength. She was a queen among women.

PERCY. Then why'd you let her get stuck with a jerk like Gabe?

POSEIDON. I thought you'd have figured that out by now. She chose to be with him, to protect you.

PERCY. Like...he has some sort of magic power?

POSEIDON. You could say that. His smell. It's so awful, no monster would ever sense you. Seriously, you've heard of Hercules and the Aegean Stables? That guy smells worse.

PERCY. I failed, Dad. The Oracle was right, I couldn't save what matters. I couldn't save Mom.

POSEIDON. You prevented a war between the gods! For that, well... The gods are unfair. But we're not total jerks.

PERCY. You mean she's...

POSEIDON. On her way. Listen, before you see her, there's something you should know. When summer ends, you can go home to her. Or you can stay at camp. Year-round.

PERCY. I didn't know I got a choice.

POSEIDON. Why do you think the gods stay out of their children's lives? The important choices are the ones you make for yourself. Still, I *am* sorry you were born.

PERCY. Wow, seriously?

POSEIDON. A hero's life is never easy.

[MUSIC 20B: REUNITED]

*(**SALLY** enters.)*

SALLY. Percy?

PERCY. Mom! You're alive!

SALLY. You saved me, baby.

PERCY. I had some help.

*(He gestures to his **FRIENDS**.)*

ANNABETH & GROVER. Hi./Hey Mrs. Jackson.

POSEIDON. *(To **SALLY**.)* Uh, hey.

*(**SALLY** notices **POSEIDON** for the first time. It's awkward...but maybe a little flirty?)*

SALLY. Hi.

POSEIDON. You look even more beautiful than the night we first met.

SALLY. You haven't changed at all.

PERCY. Okay, this is the weirdest family reunion ever.

POSEIDON. *(Awkward beat.)* My brother will want his bolt back now. Should've been the god of drama, that guy. *(He takes the backpack, then turns to* **SALLY***.)* But…I'll see you around.

*(***POSEIDON** *exits.)*

PERCY. So that's my dad.

SALLY. That's your dad.

PERCY. He told me about Gabe. Mom, you don't have to stay with him for me.

SALLY. You sound like your father. He wanted to solve all my problems too. He even offered to build me a palace under the sea. But you saved my life. It's time I figure out how to live it.

PERCY. I know you'll be strong, Mom. But if Gabe does give you any more trouble…

*(***PERCY** *hands* **SALLY** *the box.)*

SALLY. "Care of Aunty Em's Garden Emporium"?

PERCY. It's a Do-It-Yourself Sculpture Kit. *(***SALLY** *starts to open it; he stops her.)* It's Medusa's head.

ANNABETH. So what now?

PERCY. *(To* **GROVER***.)* As my official protector, you can officially escort us back to camp.

GROVER. And you're conscious this time!

(We transition to **PERCY***,* **GROVER***, and* **ANNABETH** *arriving back at camp.)*

[MUSIC 21: THE LAST DAY OF SUMMER]

PERCY. *(In his head.)*
WHAT DO YOU DO WHEN THE QUEST HAS ENDED?
WHAT DO YOU DO WHEN THE BATTLE'S WON?
SO MANY QUESTIONS LEFT UNANSWERED.
SO MANY THINGS STILL LEFT UNDONE.
AND WHAT DO YOU DO
WHEN IT'S UP TO YOU TO CHOOSE?
HAS SOMETHING ENDED OR BEGUN?
STAY OR GO?
PICK ONE.

(He shakes his unease off and follows **GROVER** *and* **ANNABETH.** *As they enter camp,* **CHIRON, LUKE,** *and* **CLARISSE** *are waiting.)*

CHIRON. I hoofed it here as soon as I heard. All hail, Perseus Jackson, hero of Olympus!

CLARISSE. Percy's alive?

ANNABETH. Hey Clarisse, we met your dad. He's not as tough as you.

CLARISSE. You met my dad? *(Then, small.)* Did he mention me?

*(***PERCY** *sees* **LUKE.***)*

PERCY. Luke! Hey… *(But* **LUKE** *walks off, ignoring him.)* Luke?

*(***PERCY** *tries to follow him, but* **MR. D** *gets in his way.)*

MR. D. Attention campers! It's the last day of summer. If you intend to make me miserable year-round, please inform us by sundown. Otherwise, the cleaning harpies will eat anyone who remains. *Perry Johanssen, this means you.*

PERCY. It's Percy Jackson!

MR. D. Whatever.

(He leaves **PERCY** *alone.)*

PERCY.

DO I STAY BECAUSE IT'S SAFER?
OR BACK TO THE HOME I LEFT BEHIND?
I COULD STAY AND TRAIN FOR A PIECE OF THE ACTION.
BUT WHAT ABOUT PEACE OF MIND?
GAH, WHAT'S MY DEAL?
WHY DO I FEEL
THERE'S SOMETHING LEFT I STILL NEED TO FIND?

(A flurry of activity: **CAMPERS** *packing and saying goodbye, etc.)*

WHERE DO YOU GO
WHEN IT'S OVER?

PERCY & CAMPERS.

WHAT DO YOU DO
WHEN YOU'VE COME
TO THE LAST DAY OF SUMMER?

*(***ANNABETH** *brings* **PERCY** *a letter.)*

ANNABETH. Hey! It's a letter from your mom.

PERCY. And a photo of her new sculpture. *(Off the photo caption.)* "Bean. Dip." *(Beat, to* **ANNABETH.***)* How come you don't go home?

ANNABETH. I tried. Once. My dad couldn't deal with the monster attacks. And my stepmom couldn't deal with me. It's just asking for trouble.

PERCY. Sometimes family's worth the trouble. Believe me.

(Beat.)

ANNABETH. I...guess we both have a choice to make, Seaweed Brain.

(**PERCY** *makes his way to the lake.* **LUKE** *finds him there.)*

PERCY. Luke!

LUKE. If it isn't the big hero.

PERCY. I've barely seen you since I got back. You avoiding me?

LUKE. *(Half-beat.)* Not at all. Tough last day?

PERCY. I thought when I finished my quest, everything would make sense. But it doesn't. I never found out who was working with Ares, or what any of this has to do with Kronos. It's the last day of summer but I don't feel like anything's over.

LUKE. I get it. My quest was supposed to be the biggest thing in my life. I came back changed. But the rest of camp was exactly the same

CHIRON ALWAYS SAYS OUR PARENTS
MADE CAMP AS THIS "SAFE MAGIC SPACE."
THE TRUTH: IT'S SO THEY DON'T HAVE TO SEE US.
THEY WON'T BOTHER TO SHOW THEIR FACE!
IT'S TIME TO MAKE THE WORLD OUR OWN,
TIME SOMEONE PUT THEM IN THEIR PLACE!

Ares thought we were starting a war between the gods. But it was bigger than that. It was about wiping them out – and taking our turn.

PERCY. *(Realizes.)* You're the lightning thief.

(**PERCY** *draws his sword;* **LUKE** *draws his.)*

LUKE. The Oracle warned you. "Betrayed by a friend."

PERCY. You set me up. *You* told me to go to the Underworld, then you gave me those shoes to pull me into that pit. You were trying to free Kronos! *Why?*

LUKE. He's promised me the power to defeat our parents.

PERCY. He's using you! To get back at the gods!

LUKE. *Good!*

I'VE BEEN HERE SINCE I WAS A KID.
I DID EV'RYTHING THEY EVER ASKED,
YEAH, I DID
AND FOR WHAT?

LUKE.	**CAMPERS.**
YOU KNOW THIS WORLD WILL NEVER BE OURS	WHAT DO YOU DO
AS LONG AS OUR PARENTS RULE OVER THE STARS.	ON THE LAST DAY OF SUMMER?
SO I'LL DO ANYTHING	SUMMER,
I DON'T CARE IF I HURT ANYONE.	SUMMER,
IT DOESN'T PAY TO BE A GOOD KID	SUMMER,
A GOOD KID	SUMMER,
A GOOD SON.	SUMMER,
THE GODS ARE NEVER ON OUR SIDE	*(Continue chanting.)*

LUKE.

SO, I THINK IT'S TIME WE WATCH THEM FALL.
AND SOON YOU'LL SEE WHAT I DID.
SOON THEY'LL BE NO GODS AT ALL!

(By now, the whole camp has entered to hear this: **ANNABETH, GROVER, SILENA, CLARISSE,** *and* **CHIRON.***)*

ANNABETH. Luke. What are you doing?

LUKE. What we promised. We said we'd never forget Thalia. *(To the* **HALF-BLOODS.***)* Join me. We'll make the gods pay for what they did to her. To all of us.

PERCY. They've made mistakes! It doesn't mean we have to make them too.

LUKE. I know you'll choose wisely, Annabeth.

ANNABETH. You're right.

*(**ANNABETH** moves to **LUKE**'s side. **LUKE** smiles – until she disarms him.)*

It's over, Luke.

LUKE. It's not over yet. Well, it is for Percy.

*(He pulls out a knife – fans know it's called Backbiter – and stabs **PERCY** in the shoulder.)*

PERCY. Ow!

ANNABETH. Percy!

*(**PERCY** falls as **LUKE** flees. **ANNABETH** and the other **CAMPERS** gather around the unconscious **PERCY**.)*

CHIRON. *(To **GROVER**, re: **LUKE**.)* Go after him!

*(**GROVER** runs after **LUKE**.)*

ANNABETH. He needs ambrosia! It's the only thing that will heal him.

*(**CHIRON** brings ambrosia over and **ANNABETH** feeds it to **PERCY**.)*

Seaweed Brain?

*(A beat. It really seems like **PERCY** is a goner. Finally, **PERCY** opens his eyes.)*

PERCY. Wise girl?

*(They move in close. Are they going to kiss? We never find out, because **GROVER** re-enters.)*

GROVER. He's gone. But he won't get far. I'll have all the squirrels on the east coast searching for him.

ANNABETH. He'll be back.

CLARISSE. Then he'll be sorry.

CHIRON. This won't end with Luke. We stand on the brink of dangerous times, for gods *and* mortals. I can't tell you what to do. But if you choose to remain here, know that you'll have the full protection of the gods.

PERCY. No. Luke was right about one thing. We can't hide at camp waiting for our parents to fix things. We have to do it ourselves – out there, in the real world. That's where the monsters are.

ANNABETH. The gods will say we're impertinent.

PERCY. We *are* impertinent.

[MUSIC 22: BRING ON THE MONSTERS]

THERE'S GONNA BE A FIGHT.
THERE STILL MIGHT BE A WAR.
FOR THE MOMENT WE GOT
DANGER ON THE RUN.

ANNABETH.

AND THINGS'LL GET BAD,
BEFORE THEY WILL GET BETTER.
IT MAY FEEL LIKE AN ENDING
BUT THE BATTLE'S JUST BEGUN.

GROVER.

ARE WE EVER GONNA
ONCE HAVE IT EASY?

PERCY.

NOPE!
FEELIN' READY.

ANNABETH.
FEELIN' STOKED.

GROVER.
FEELIN' QUEASY.

ANNABETH.
WE COULD FAIL BUT WE HAVE TO TRY.

PERCY.
DON'T FEEL BAD,
'CAUSE WE'RE USUALLY ABOUT TO DIE!

PERCY, ANNABETH & GROVER.
BRING ON THE MONSTERS.
BRING ON THE MONSTERS.
BRING ON THE REAL WORLD.
BRING ON THE MONSTERS.

ALL CAMPERS.
BRING ON THE REAL WORLD.

CHIRON.
THEY'LL BE TIMES WHEN YOUR FAITH IS SHAKEN.

SILENA.
THEY'RE BREAKIN' YOUR HEART?
THEN TRY TO HEAR IT POUND.

CLARISSE & ANNABETH. *(To each other.)*
GOTTA KNOW WHERE THE REAL FIGHT LIES.

ANNABETH.
WHEN IT'S TIME TO RISE AND STAND YOUR GROUND.

GROVER.
WE DON'T HAVE TO GO IT ALONE.

CLARISSE.
THEY'LL PUT US IN A BOX,
BUT WE WON'T BE CONTAINED.

ANNABETH.

YOU KEEP HOPIN.'
YOU KEEP YOUR EYES OPEN.

PERCY.

'CAUSE THE SEA DOESN'T LIKE TO BE RESTRAINED.

ALL.

NO, I'M NEVER GONNA
ONCE HAVE IT EASY.
I'LL MAKE MISTAKES,
BUT MY OWN,
AND IT FREES ME.
SUMMER'S OVER,
IT'S TIME TO BEGIN.

PERCY, ANNABETH & GROVER.

AND IF YOU'RE LOOKIN' FOR TROUBLE
THEN.

ALL.

COUNT ME IN!
BRING ON THE MONSTERS.
BRING ON THE MONSTERS.
BRING ON THE REAL WORLD.
BRING ON THE MONSTERS.

PERCY.

BRING ON THE REAL WORLD!

PERCY.	**CHORUS.**
BRING ON THE REAL WORLD	AH
BRING ON THE REAL WORLD.	AH
THE REAL WORLD.	AH
AND I'LL BE BACK NEXT SUMMER,	AH
YOU'LL SEE ME AGAIN.	
I'LL BE BACK NEXT SUMMER	
I'LL SURVIVE 'TIL THEN.	

I'LL BE BACK NEXT SUMMER, AH
YOU'LL SEE ME AGAIN.
I'LL BE BACK NEXT SUMMER,
I'LL BE BACK NEXT SUMMER

PERCY.	ANNABETH.
I'LL BE BACK NEXT SUMMER,	BRING ON THE REAL WORLD.

PERCY.	GROVER.
YOU'LL SEE ME AGAIN,	DRIVE, JUST DRIVE.

PERCY.	ANNABETH.	GROVER.
I'LL BE BACK NEXT SUMMER	BRING ON THE REAL WORLD	STAY AHEAD, AND STAY AHEAD

PERCY.	GROVER.
I'LL SURVIVE 'TIL THEN.	AND STAY ALIVE!

PERCY.
I'LL BE BACK NEXT SUMMER,

PERCY.	ANNABETH & CLARISSE.	SILENA & CHIRON.
YOU'LL SEE ME AGAIN.	BRING ON THE REAL WORLD.	NORMAL IS A MYTH.

PERCY.
I'LL BE BACK NEXT SUMMER,
I'LL BE BACK NEXT SUMMER.

PERCY.	ANNABETH.	CAMPERS.
I'LL BE BACK NEXT SUMMER,	BRING ON THE REAL WORLD.	WE'LL MAKE 'EM LISTEN TO US.

PERCY.
YOU'LL SEE ME AGAIN,

CAMPERS.
WE'LL MAKE 'EM LISTEN.

PERCY.
I'LL BE BACK NEXT SUMMER,

ANNABETH.
BRING ON ANY CHAL-LENGE.

CAMPERS.
WE'LL MAKE 'EM LISTEN TO US.

PERCY.
I'LL SURVIVE 'TIL THEN.

CAMPERS.
WE'LL MAKE 'EM LISTEN, OH.

PERCY.
I'LL BE BACK NEXT SUMMER,

ANNABETH.
BRING ON THE REAL WORLD.

CAMPERS.
WE'LL MAKE 'EM LISTEN TO US.

PERCY.
YOU'LL SEE ME AGAIN.

CAMPERS.
WE'LL MAKE 'EM LISTEN.

PERCY.
I'LL BE BACK NEXT SUMMER,
I'LL BE BACK NEXT SUMMER.

[MUSIC 23: BOWS / EXIT MUSIC]

The End

www.ingramcontent.com/pod-product-compliance
Ingram Content Group UK Ltd.
Pitfield, Milton Keynes, MK11 3LW, UK
UKHW021839190325
456484UK00002B/2

9 780573 709180